Arianne's captor tore away his coif and pulled the mail from his head, revealing his identity.

"Richard!" she gasped and nearly fell back against the pallet.

"The very same, milady," he chuckled. "The one whom the world's armies could not defeat."

Arianne felt the realization of safety coursing through her veins. Richard reached forward and cut the bonds from her hands and feet. Shock numbed her mind, and Arianne did nothing for a moment but stare in mute surprise.

"Are you injured, Arianne?" Richard questioned, reaching out to touch her hand. He took her fingers in his mailed hand and noticed the cuts and dried blood. He frowned, feeling an anger beyond all that he'd known before.

"What other suffering have you endured?" he questioned, praying that God had been merciful to his young wife.

Dropping her hands, Richard reached for the light and brought it closer. When it shone full upon her face, Richard could see the dark bruise on her jaw. With an anguished cry, he ripped off his mail gloves and took Arianne's face in his hands.

"What has he done to you?"

TRACIE J. PETERSON is a popular inspirational writer and a regular columnist for a Christian newspaper in Topeka, Kansas. Tracie has also written eight successful **Heartsong Presents** titles under the name of Janelle Jamison.

HEARTSONG PRESENTS

Books under the pen name of Janelle Jamison.

HP19—A Place to Belong
HP40—Perfect Love
HP47—Tender Journeys
HP56—A Light in the Window
HP63—The Willing Heart
HP71—Destiny's Road
HP88—Beyond Today
HP93—Iditarod Dream

Books by Tracie J. Peterson.

HP102—If Given a Choice

Don't miss out on any of our super romances. Write to us at the following address for information on our newest releases and club information.

Heartsong Presents Readers' Service
P.O. Box 719
Uhrichsville, OH 44683

A Kingdom
Divided

Tracie J. Peterson

Heartsong Presents

To Steve Reginald,
my editor and friend,
with thanks for the help you've offered,
the direction you've given,
and the chances you've taken with my work.
Philippians 1:3
sums it up from me to you.

A note from the Author:
I love to hear from my readers! You may correspond
with me by writing:

Tracie J. Peterson
Author Relations
P.O. Box 719
Uhrichsville, OH 44683

ISBN 1-55748-669-7

A KINGDOM DIVIDED

Copyright © 1995 by Tracie J. Peterson. All rights reserved.
Except for use in any review, the reproduction or utilization of
this work in whole or in part in any form by any electronic,
mechanical, or other means, now known or hereafter invented,
is forbidden without the permission of the publisher, Heartsong
Presents, P.O. Box 719, Uhrichsville, Ohio 44683.

All of the characters and events in this book are fictitious.
Any resemblance to actual persons, living or dead, or to
actual events is purely coincidental.

PRINTED IN THE U.S.A.

one

"I desire to see her," the tall man stated with an air of one used to his commands being met. His scowl deepened as he awaited an answer.

Duke Geoffrey Pemberton looked sternly at the speaker. It was difficult for him to take orders, much more so from one who was a score of years his junior. Still, the duke of Gavenshire, His Grace Richard DuBonnet, was no ordinary man, and the orders he gave were nearly the same as if they'd come from King Henry himself.

"Surely it would be a waste of Your Grace's time. She is everything your proxy must have told you. I assure you, I speak for my daughter when I say she will go into this marriage with dignity, respect, and honor," Pemberton said in a much controlled manner and added, "Remember, sire, 'twas your choice to send a proxy to the betrothal ceremony."

Richard brought both fists down on the table. He was weary of dealing with the older man. Weary from the greed and unpleasant cruelties he'd witnessed in things Duke Pemberton said and did.

"Don't question me," Richard said firmly. His breeding and background had given him the skills to easily fight and defeat opponents, but he recognized that the art of diplomacy was wasted on one such as Pemberton. "I want to see her now!" he exclaimed without room for argument.

Pemberton bit back a retort and called for his daughter's chambermaid. The terrified girl appeared, cringing as the duke bellowed out the order that his daughter was to be brought at once to the great hall.

The maid curtsied to both men and, gathering her skirts, lit up the stairs as though a roaring fire chased her.

Richard eased back into the nearest chair. Cupping his hand against the neatly trimmed beard he wore, Richard's green eyes never left his host.

The man was ruthless and cruel and it showed in his dark eyes. Richard had been forewarned, not only by his men, but by the King's messengers as well. Pemberton had a reputation for a quick temper and heavy hand, which led Richard to wonder about the daughter who would soon be his wife.

Just then the frightened maid returned to curtsey again at her scowling master. "My lady is indisposed at present, sire. She begs to join you in a moment." The girl cowered awaiting an angry strike, but Pemberton noted the frown on Richard's face and held back retaliation. Before Richard could speak, Pemberton was up the stairs, disappearing from sight.

"You may go," Richard said softly and the girl hurried from the room, not even raising her eyes to acknowledge the duke's words.

❧

With brush in hand, Arianne Pemberton sat quickly stroking her long hair. The Duke of Gavenshire, her betrothed, sat in the great hall below. She'd never even met him before finding herself suddenly engaged. What manner of man would send a proxy for his betrothal ceremonies and leave his bride-to-be wondering at the sight and condition of the man she would vow to take to her side for life?

She hummed nervously to herself, then stopped with a frown. Her father, only moments ago, had sent the maid to fetch her. She had sent the maid back to decline and no doubt her father would be furious. *But I have to dress my hair,* Arianne thought. *It would have been most inappropriate to have been introduced to the duke with my head bare.*

In spite of her attempts to convince herself she'd made the right decision, the one thing that kept coming back to her was the cruelty she'd known at her father's hand. He wouldn't like her defiance, just as he hadn't cared about her feelings toward the upcoming marriage. She didn't want the wedding, but he did. That put them at odds.

Arianne continued to run the brush through her hair, even while she considered the consequences of her actions. Her father was a ruthless man who ruled all around him with a mixture of injustice and self-servitude. He would not take lightly Arianne's delay.

Arianne's door slammed abruptly open, causing her to drop her brush.

"Get thee below at once!" her father raged. He gave her no chance to stand, but reached out and yanked the girl to her feet and out the door.

Below in the great hall, Richard heard the commotion. Pemberton appeared at the top of the stairs, dragging behind a shapely young woman.

With hip-length auburn hair flying out behind her, Lady Arianne Pemberton was dragged down the steps and landed in an unceremonious heap at her father's feet.

"Here," her father said smugly, "is your bride. Her

temper can be a bit much, but the back of your hand will easily settle her disposition."

Richard was on his feet in a heartbeat and before Arianne could lift her face, he was helping her.

"Your Grace," she whispered and pushed back the wavy bulk of hair that kept her face from his. Dark brown eyes met angry green ones, causing Arianne to instantly realize that her worst fears had come true. She was to marry a man just like her father!

"Milady," Richard spoke softly, delivering her to a nearby chair. Turning abruptly, Richard closed the distance to where the duke stood with a haughty stare of disgust.

Balling his hand into a fist, Richard raised it to within inches of the duke's face. "Never, I repeat, never treat my wife with such ill-respect again or you will feel the consequences of your actions."

Arianne could not suppress a gasp of surprise. No one had ever dared to speak to her father in such a manner. The duke's face flamed red, but he remained silent, further surprising his daughter. He must want this match badly.

With the King's edict that she be wed to the duke of Gavenshire, Arianne couldn't imagine that her father would worry that the marriage wouldn't take place. Perhaps he was simply in awe of the younger man's position with the King. Arianne knew that position and power were the only things of importance to her father and surmised that this must, indeed, be the reason for his good manners.

Completely ignoring the indignant duke, Richard turned to take in the vision of the woman he was slated to spend all of time with. She was everything his men had related and more. They hadn't told him of the way her hair flashed glints of gold amidst the deep auburn mass. No doubt they'd not seen her hair, Richard mused, for it would have been covered with a white linen wimple and mantel.

Arianne grew uncomfortable under the duke's close scrutiny. She'd had no time to plait her hair and cover her head before her father had stormed into her chamber and dragged her to meet her husband-to-be. She was most grateful that she'd dressed carefully in forest green velvet, for while it was simply adorned with a gold and jeweled belt at her waist, it was a becoming color and Arianne did hope to meet with the duke's approval.

"Milady," Richard said, coming to greet her formally, "I am Richard DuBonnet, duke of Gavenshire." He gave a bit of a bow before taking Arianne's hand in his own and continuing. "And you, of course, are the most lovely Lady Arianne Pemberton."

Arianne wanted to melt into the rush-covered floor. The warmth in his eyes set her heart beating faster, but the gentleness of his touch was as none she'd ever known.

"Your Grace," she whispered, getting to her feet. Even as she curtsied deeply, Richard refused to let go of her hand.

"It would pleasure me greatly, milady, if you were to call meRichard."

Arianne rose and lifted her face to his. "Richard," she whispered the name, trembling from head to toe.

"And might I call you Arianne?" he questioned. Both of them were oblivious to the older duke, staring on in complete loathing of the gentle exchange.

"But of course, Your—Richard," Arianne corrected

herself. She mustn't do anything to anger this powerful man. "You may call me whatever pleases you."

A hint of a smile played at the corners of Richard's lips. "It pleases me to call you my wife," he said boldly. "The King has chosen well for me."

Arianne blushed scarlet and felt her knees grow weak. She couldn't very well reply with her true feelings toward the arrangement. Not with such gallant praise being issued on her behalf. With a quick glance past Richard to where her father stood, Arianne realized instantly that he was displeased.

Richard noticed the exchange at once and led Arianne back to the chair. "Come, we will speak of our marriage," he announced.

Duke Pemberton could no longer remain silent. "I see no need to waste your valuable time, Your Grace. You must have many affairs to oversee. I have already assured you of my daughter's virtue, dowry—"

"Yes, yes. I know all about the business dealings of my betrothal and marriage. What I desire to know now is the heart of your daughter," Richard interrupted with a flash of anger in his eyes.

"But what woman knows her heart on any matter?" Pemberton retorted with a silencing stare directed at his daughter. "Her thoughts are nothing to you or to me. She knows how to tend a household and direct the running of an estate. She is a comely lass and no doubt will give you many fine sons. More than this is unimportant."

Arianne knew better than to cross her father. She was not yet married, and until she came under Richard's complete protection there was always the possibility that her father would beat her for her remarks. She shuddered, knowing that she still bore lash marks from the last argument she'd had with her father regarding the upcoming marriage.

Richard took the seat beside Arianne and stared thoughtfully at the duke as if he considered his words of value. Then without warning, he turned to her. "What are your thoughts on the matter of our marriage, Arianne?"

Arianne's father seethed noticeably at the disregard of his statement. He flashed a warning to Arianne that told of trouble to come should she say anything to jeopardize her standing in this arrangement.

Arianne bowed her head slightly before speaking. "It is my honor to share vows with you." The words were barely audible.

"You know very little of me," Richard continued gently. "Is there something I might share with you regarding myself that would put to rest any questionable matter in your mind?"

"Nay, Your Grace," she replied, forgetting to call him Richard.

"Is there any matter about yourself, which you would like to share with me?" he questioned.

Arianne was shaking noticeably now. On one side stood her father, threatening with his eyes to strip her of her dignity should she say anything outside of his instruction and on the other side was Richard, who genuinely seemed to care about her feelings.

The room grew uncomfortably silent. The tension between the girl and her father was clear. Richard frowned slightly. He noticed Arianne's trembling and the duke's scowling face. So long as the Arianne's father remained within sight, she would no doubt say little or nothing.

Without warning, Richard stood and pointed to the door. "Leave us," he commanded the duke.

Pemberton was shocked beyond reason and enraged beyond words. He struggled for the right response, but before he could find any words, Richard called for his men and ordered them to take the duke into the outer room.

Richard knew he was making a great enemy, but he no longer cared. His real concern was for the frightened young woman who sat cringing in terror.

As his men took the Duke from the room, Richard called out one final order. "We are not to be disturbed for any reason."

When the door closed behind his men, Richard turned to Arianne and smiled. "Now, Arianne, you must feel free to speak to me honestly."

Arianne's mouth dropped open slightly and Richard couldn't help but notice her lips. Raising his gaze slightly, he stared into huge brown eyes that reminded him hauntingly of a doe about to be slain.

"I. . .I. . .," she stammered for words.

Richard sat back down and took her hand in his own. Lifting it to his lips, he gently kissed the back. "Arianne," he whispered, "I can read things in your eyes that are not making their way to your lips. You might as well speak your heart. You aren't going to offend or injure me, I assure you. Now speak to me of this marriage. Are you truly in agreement?" he questioned gently.

Arianne could feel the warmth of his breath against her hand and pulled it back quickly. "I have never been allowed the luxury of speaking openly, sire—Richard."

"I'm certain you speak the truth," he said with a slight

smile. "But your father is no longer a concern to you. You are under my protection and you will leave with me on the 'morrow, so put aside your fears and talk to me. We cannot change what the King has arranged, but we might yet come to a better understanding of it."

Arianne swallowed the lump in her throat. She lifted her delicate face to meet Richard's gentle expression. With the exception of her brother Devon, she'd never known a man such as Richard. But Devon was hundreds, maybe even thousands of miles away doing the King's bidding, just as she was doing the royal bidding at home.

"I am against marriage to you," she said softly, then tightly shut her eyes and braced herself for his rage.

"I see," he replied without emotion. "Has another captured your affections?"

Arianne's eyes snapped open. "Nay, there is no other," she stated adamantly.

"Then what makes this arrangement so unbearable?"

"I. . .I," she stammered for a moment then drew a deep breath. "I do not love you, Richard."

Richard chuckled.

"You laugh at me?" Arianne quickly questioned.

"Nay, dear lady. I do not laugh at you. Neither do I expect you to love me. Not yet, anyway. We've only just met and this arrangement is new to both of us." Richard paused, getting to his feet. He paced a few steps before continuing.

"Why, in all honesty, I hadn't planned to take a wife, at least not yet. When King Henry suggested this arrangement, however, I knew it would be one that would benefit our families and fulfill his desire to see me properly wed."

Richard's words seemed most sincere and Arianne

began to relax. Perhaps the duke was not the kind of man her father was.

Arianne studied Richard for a moment. He was handsome—tall and lean with broad shoulders. His legs were heavily muscled, no doubt from many hours of supporting the chain mail hauberk and chaussures that were customary costume for men of armor. His dark brown hair had been neatly trimmed, as had been his mustache and beard. But most disturbing were his eyes; green eyes so fiery one minute and soft, almost child-like, the next. Arianne truly wished she knew more about the duke of Gavenshire.

"It is a good arrangement for my family," Arianne finally spoke. "I would never do anything to disgrace them. Neither would I do anything to bring the King's wrath upon them. It is my desire to be married to you, just as King Henry wishes."

Richard stopped in his pace and turned. "I don't wish to force an undesirable union upon you, Arianne. The church still presses its people for mutual consent to marriage. I could speak to the King, if it is your wish that we discontinue these arrangements."

"Nay!" Arianne exclaimed coming up out of her seat. She threw herself at Richard's feet. Her father would kill her for causing the betrothal to be dissolved. Under no circumstances could she appear to be anything but congenial. "Please don't!" There were tears in her eyes. "I beg of you!"

Richard lifted her from the floor and set her down in front of him. "Arianne, you mustn't worry. I understand your circumstances. If you are truly agreed, I want very much for this wedding to take place."

Arianne nodded, unmindful of the tears that streamed down her cheeks. "I am agreed, sire. I will make you a good wife. I promise."

"I've no doubt about that," Richard stated. He reached up to wipe away the tears on her face. "I simply want you to be happy, as well."

Arianne's heart soared, and the first spark of feeling for her soon-to-be husband was born. "I will be happy, Richard, and in time, I pray it will be God's will that I grow to love you."

two

Without a chance for her father to lay a hand to her again, Arianne found herself in a long traveling procession the very next morning. She mused over the events that had led to this day. Everyone had been stunned when the young duke, himself, had arrived to bring the party to his castle. But even more surprising was the way he'd taken control of His Grace, Geoffrey Pemberton. Even Arianne was amazed.

Arianne had never understood what her father expected to gain from her match with the duke of Gavenshire. Of course it bode well to have such a powerful man in one's family lineage, but Arianne also knew that her father was giving up a great portion of estates that adjoined Richard's property. It was part of her dowry, and Arianne was hard pressed to understand how her father would have ever conceded to such an arrangement. The King must have promised him a great deal more than what he stood to lose.

Upon her own fine mare, Arianne enjoyed the passing warmth of the afternoon sun. Soon they would stop for the night, and the next day they would make their way to Gavenshire castle.

Absorbed in thought, Arianne did not hear the rider approach to join her. Richard held back in silence, taking in the beauty he found before him. She sat regally, he thought, and in truth he had always wondered how a woman could sit so confidently atop a sidesaddle. Arianne, however, seemed not to consider the situation. She was like a child taking in the countryside around her. A look of awe was fixed upon her face.

"Does the ride overtax you, milady?"

Arianne jerked back on the reins without thought. "My pardon, sire. You startled me." She released the reins and allowed the horse to proceed. "What was it you asked of me?"

Richard smiled. "I asked if the ride overtaxed you."

"Nay," Arianne replied with a wistful look spreading across her face. "In truth it is something wondrous. I have never known the land outside a half-day's ride from my home. The world is much larger out here."

Richard laughed heartily. "That it is, Arianne."

Arianne fixed her eyes boldly on Richard for a moment, and with her smile deepening added, "There is much that I have to learn." The depths of her brown eyes pulled at Richard's heart.

He leaned forward and in hardly more than a whisper spoke. "It would pleasure me greatly to be your teacher."

Arianne blushed deeply at what could seemingly have been a statement of mixed meaning. Had he thought her a flirt? Before she could speak, one of Richard's men hailed him from the front of the procession and Richard bid her farewell.

That night, it seemed Arianne's eyes had barely closed in sleep before she was being urged awake. Today they would reach Gavenshire, she thought, and hastened her steps to get dressed.

She had prepared for this day with great care. Calling the servants her father had allowed her to borrow for the journey, Arianne directed and ordered each one until everything was just as she desired. Too nervous to eat anything, Arianne sent her breakfast away without so much as touching a crumb.

Donning a delicate tunic of pale, lavender silk, Arianne nodded her approval and turned to be fitted in the surcoat of samite. The samite blend of wool and silk had been dyed deep purple and trimmed in ermine. Arianne had no desire to appear a pauper before her husband's people.

Within the hour, Arianne's toilette was complete, and she was seated once again on her side saddle. She glanced around nervously for Richard and blushed deeply when she met his open stare of approval. With long easy strides he came to where her mare pranced anxiously.

"Lady Arianne," he said taking her hand to his lips, "you are the epitome of that which all English women should strive for. Your beauty blinds me to all else."

"Your Grace," she whispered, then corrected herself. "I mean, Richard." She seemed at a loss as to how she should respond to his flattery.

"I trust you slept well," the duke responded before she had a chance to concern herself overmuch.

"Aye," she said with a nod. "Albeit a short rest, 'twas quite refreshing."

"Good," Richard said with a smile. "Then we will be on our way. Gavenshire and her people await their new duchess."

Although Arianne had lived a life of ease compared to many, she was dumbly silent at the vision of Gavenshire Castle. The grey stone walls stood atop the cliffs, rising majestically above the background of the sea's churning waters.

She gasped in awe as they drew ever closer. The spiraling twin towers of the castle seemed to dwarf the village at its feet. Everywhere, brightly colored banners flew in celebration of her marriage to the duke of Gavenshire.

If the castle was not enough, Arianne was absolutely stunned when people lined every inch of the roadway in order to get a look at their soon-to-be duchess.

The crowd cheered, while peasants handed up flowers to her waiting hands. Arianne beamed smiles upon everyone, which prompted even greater response. She was a bit afraid of the sea of people at her side, but Richard had not returned to assist her and so Arianne had to believe that nothing was amiss and that she should enjoy this as her special moment with his people.

Just then, a small girl darted out in front of Arianne's mare, causing the horse to rear. Arianne tightened her grip and leaned into the horse's neck. She soothed the horse into stillness, while the child's mother ran forward to claim her frightened daughter.

"A thousand pardons, milady. The child meant no harm, she's just excited by the noise and celebration," the woman stated as if fearing for the life of the child she now held. The crowd around them fell silent and waited for their new duchess to act.

Arianne smiled. "Your apology is unwarranted, Madam. I, myself, am quite caught up in the revelry as well."

A cheer went up once again and Arianne could feel the mare begin to shift in nervous agitation. Soothing the horse with a gentle stroke, Arianne reached down and gave the child a quick pat on the head and moved the horse forward.

Richard observed the incident from where he'd brought

his mount to a stop. Arianne was truly a remarkable woman. In one simple act of kindness she had sealed herself upon the hearts of his people.

The sun broke out from clouds overhead, and flashed out across the earth, touching everything in its warmth. Arianne lifted her face for a moment to catch the rays, and as she lowered her eyes, she caught sight of Richard. The look he gave her was so intimate that she quickly looked away. What manner of man was the duke of Gavenshire that he would boldly assess his wife in public?

The days that followed, did so with such momentum that Arianne was left breathless at the end of each one. There was her introduction to the castle, which though thorough, left her more puzzled than ever. She comforted herself in the knowledge that exploration and understanding would come later.

The wedding itself, planned by the duke and his household, was more elaborate than Arianne had ever dreamed. The celebrating and festivities would most likely continue for yet another week.

The day of their wedding was perfect. The church at Gavenshire welcomed the duke and his duchess and all who could crowd inside to share in the pledges of matrimony.

Arianne wore her finest clothes. A linen chemise of pale gold with an exquisite tunic of burgundy silk adorned her frame. Over this came a surcoat of dark gold velvet which had been lavishly embroidered and trimmed in fur. At Richard's request, she had left her hair unplaited, a most unusual thing but one which seemed only to enhance her beauty. On her head she wore a veil of gossamer gold that shimmered in the light when she walked. It was held in place by a narrow gold band that glittered from the three stones it held: a diamond, a ruby, and an emerald.

Richard nodded his heartfelt approval as she approached the priest with him. The priest bade them join right hands, and when Arianne touched Richard's large warm hand with her own small trembling one, peace settled over her.

They repeated their vows before God, the church, and their people and waited while the priest expounded on the virtues of religious education, a tranquil home, and a pure marriage bed.

Finally he asked for the ring, which Richard promptly produced. The priest blessed the ring, then handed it back to Richard. Arianne noted that it looked to be a small replica of the band which held her veil in place.

"In the name of the Father," Richard whispered and slipped the ring on Arianne's index finger, "And of the Son," he continued and slipped it to the second finger. "And of the Holy Ghost," he fitted it to the third finger. "With this ring I thee wed."

Arianne thought she might actually faint. The moment was so intense, so intimate, that she could scarcely draw a breath. The ceremony continued and finally after the nuptial mass, Richard received the kiss of peace from the priest and turned to pass it to his new wife.

Gently he lifted Arianne's veil and smiled. Her brown eyes were huge in anticipation, melting Richard's heart and resolve. He leaned forward without reaching out to her otherwise and, for the first time, touched his lips to hers. He'd only intended to linger a moment, but it was as if he were held against his will. The kiss deepened until without thought, Richard had gripped

Arianne's shoulders.

A gentle cough by the priest told Richard that the marriage was sealed sufficiently. Sheepishly, Richard pulled back with a half-apologetic, half-frustrated look on his face before taking Arianne's hand. He led her quietly from the church to the waiting crowd. They were heralded by the people with such sincere warmth and joy that Arianne could not keep the tears from her eyes.

"What be this?" Richard questioned, reaching out to touch a single drop against her cheek. "You are not already regretting this union, are you?"

"Nay, Richard," Arianne whispered against his bent head. "I am moved beyond thought at the kindness of your people."

Richard lifted her hand to his lips and gave it a squeeze. "They do love you, Duchess."

If the revelry prior to the ceremony was impressive, then the celebration which followed in the great hall of Gavenshire Castle was extraordinary.

First there were the tables laden with food of every imaginable kind. Huge roasted legs of beef were set before them on gold platters, while baked capons, chickens, and rabbits were arranged on smaller plates. Fruits, vegetables, sweetmeats, and breads filled numerous bowls and platters in a nearly endless display of prosperity.

Arianne sat at Richard's side, sharing with him a common chalice and water bowl. When Arianne inadvertently placed her hand on the goblet at the same time Richard reached for it, the intimacy seemed too much. The warmth of his hand covered hers as he lifted the glass to her lips first and then his own. Those at the table who witnessed the act roared in hearty approval and predicted that many would be the number of sons born to this union.

Arianne grew apprehensive and could not look Richard in the eye. She hadn't wanted this marriage, yet it was impossible to deny that he was kind and gentle with her. She thought of the night to come and nearly grimaced while taking a mouthful of roasted boar. She had always hoped that she could give herself in marriage to a man that she cared for, nay, loved. It wasn't uncommon that people sought that affection, but in a world where the destiny of one usually correlated to the desires of others, Arianne knew that she'd been most fortunate to end up married to a man such as Richard DuBonnet. She could only pray that love would come.

The festivities continued with jongleurs playing lively songs upon their lutes and viols. A man with a tabor played, while another man sang the words of a love song written on behalf of Arianne. He sang of her beauty and virtue, while most of the hall fell silent in awe.

Arianne herself was moved to tears, but she quickly held them in check. She had never felt such warmth and caring from anyone in her life.

Soon the tables were moved aside and dancing took place. The people's merriment for the day was evident in the whirling and clapping that accompanied the dance. Arianne found herself passed among Richard's knights and one after the other whirled, lifted, and paraded her across the floor with great flourish. She caught sight of her father and Richard only once, but it was enough of a glimpse to tell her that Richard was unhappy with the older man.

Finally the revelry grew somber again and the tables were set with supper. The priest blessed the meal and the

house, then placed his hands upon Richard and Arianne
and blessed their union once again. He added a blessing
for the nuptial bed before releasing them to the feast, causing Arianne to blush deeply.

Arianne found eating impossible. She picked at a piece
of chicken unmercifully until Richard finally put his hand
upon hers and stilled her attack.

"I have a gift for you," he said softly. Richard turned
and motioned to an older woman. Arianne lifted her face
to find a radiant smile and soft grey eyes.

"This is Matilda," Richard said. "She will be your lady's
maid." Without a word being spoken, Arianne immediately liked the woman. Something in her countenance
bespoke loyalty and friendship, maybe even the motherly
love that Arianne had been robbed of at an early age.

"Matilda," Arianne tried the name. "I am pleased to
have your care."

"As am I, to care for you, milady," Matilda replied.

Before anything else was said, Richard leaned toward
the two women. "Arianne, Matilda will take you to my,
our chamber. Perhaps you will feel better away from this
crowd. I will join you later."

Arianne nodded without meeting Richard's eyes.
Matilda was to prepare her for her wedding bed as was
the custom of the bride's mother. Gently rising, Arianne
followed Matilda from the room amidst the roars and calls
of some of the heartier knights. Richard's men intended
that he be embarrassed, but he only frowned, knowing
the likely uneasiness it caused Arianne.

Upstairs, Arianne permitted Matilda's service, while
the woman spoke of the castle and Richard.

"I've know him since he was in swaddling, milady,"

Matilda said. She gently removed the heavy belt and surcoat from Arianne. "He is a good master and never a kinder one was born."

Arianne smiled at the woman's obvious devotion. "What of his family?" she questioned. "I've met no one who lays claim to his blood."

Matilda frowned momentarily. "His Grace doesn't allow anyone to speak of them, but I knew them well. I cared for his mother."

Arianne waited while Matilda finished removing the tunic and chemise. She accepted a soft shift of pale cream silk before speaking again to Matilda.

"Is there bad blood between Richard and his family, Matilda?"

"Nay, mistress. 'Tis no small matter to deal with either, and I would not betray my master by speaking of it." Matilda's words were firm, but she sought to ease Arianne's fearful stare by continuing with stories of Richard as a boy.

Arianne allowed the woman to direct her to a chair, where Matilda brushed her hair until each coppery lock seemed to blaze under the soft glow of candlelight. When the task was completed, Matilda stoked the fire in the hearth and built it up until it was a cheerful blaze. Then she extinguished the candles and took her leave.

Arianne drew her legs up to her chest and tucked the silken garment around her feet. She finally allowed herself to gaze around the room, taking in first the fire, then the shadowy forms of clothing chests, and finally the huge bed that she was to share with her husband.

The bed, half again as long as a man's height was nearly as wide across. Overhead the massive wood canopy was decorated with intricate carvings and rich velvet curtains. It was no pauper's bed, to be sure.

Just then the door opened and against the dim light of the hallway, Richard's well-muscled frame stood fast. He stared at his wife. A more heavenly vision he could not imagine, but even from across the room he could see that she trembled. He slowly closed the door and set the bar in place.

"You are beautiful, Arianne," he whispered, coming to the fireplace. "I am a most blessed man."

Arianne lifted her eyes, meeting the passionate look of her husband. Words stuck in her throat. What should she say? What could she?

Richard wished nothing more than to dispel the fear in her eyes. Fear that he knew held deep root in her heart.

"I was sorry that your brother couldn't attend the wedding," he said, taking a seat on the bed opposite where she sat. "I know very little about you," he continued. "I would be most honored if you would speak to me about your youth."

Arianne relaxed a bit. Richard seemed content to sit apart from her, and his words made her realize that he had no intention of rushing the night.

"My mother died when I was but six years old," Arianne finally spoke. "I remember only little things about her because I was quickly taken off to a convent where I was schooled and held until my father's instruction. My brother, Devon, would visit me often there. We are very close," she said with a sadness to her voice that Richard wished he could cast out.

"My father returned me home when my brother Devon was preparing to ride with the King's men. We shared only a few short months before Devon left, and I have not seen him since. That was five years ago."

"And in all that time he's not returned home?" Richard questioned.

"He and my father are at odds," Arianne whispered. "It seems my father finds a rival in everything."

"Aye," Richard murmured, "I can vouch for that."

"I pray my father has not overly grieved you," Arianne replied.

Richard shook his head and reached out a hand to touch her. Arianne instantly recoiled back into the chair. She regretted the action, but could do nothing to take it back.

Richard saw the fear return to her eyes and sighed. "Arianne, I'm no monster. I will not beat and abuse you as others must have done. You have nothing to fear from me."

Arianne tried to steady her nerves. Her heart raced at a murderous pace and she found that fear gripped her throat.

Richard got up and pulled Arianne to her feet. "I will not press you to consummate this marriage," he said firmly. "In fact, I will not seal this arrangement until there is no longer fear in your eyes and heart toward me."

Arianne felt the warmth of his touch spread down her arms. "I will not deny you," she whispered.

"Yea, but I will deny myself," Richard replied. "I have but one request in return."

"Name it, sire."

"That you share my bed upon my honor that I will not touch you," he replied. Then with eyes twinkling and a slight smile upon his lips he corrected himself. "Nay, I would hold you, but demand nothing more."

Arianne nodded slowly, still amazed that he would do

such a thing for her. She cast her glance from Richard's face to the bed and back again when a horrible thought gripped her mind.

"The virginal sheets," she whispered.

"The what? What are you talking about, Arianne?"

"The virginal sheets." Her voice trembled. "Without them, I'll be shamed and so will you."

Richard stared blankly for a moment and then recalled the barbaric custom of a bride's proof of virtue. He grimaced slightly. "I'm sorry, milady. I forgot." Then turning to the bed he yanked down the coverlets and pointed. "Lie down."

Arianne steadied her nerves and straightened her shoulders. *This is it*, she thought, and even though Richard had promised to wait, she quietly obeyed his command.

She closed her eyes as she reclined on the cold sheets. With her fists clenched at her sides and jaws tight, Arianne waited.

Richard stared down at her shapely form with more compassion for her fear than he'd ever known for anyone. "Open your eyes, Arianne," he said after several moments.

Arianne forced herself to look at Richard. In her eyes was the look of a trapped animal and Richard longed to end her suffering and ease her fears.

"Now, get up," he whispered and extended a hand to help her. Arianne was stunned but nevertheless scooted quickly from the bed to stand beside her husband.

With one fluid motion, Richard drew a jeweled ceremonial dagger from his belt and slashed his forearm with a small stroke.

Arianne gasped aloud at the crimson stain that appeared

on Richard's arm. He never took his eyes from her face as he waited calmly for the blood to pool. Then walking to where Arianne had lain, he sprinkled his blood over the sheet.

"There," he said with a sheepish grin. "The virginal sheets."

Arianne stood open-mouthed, staring at her husband. "Why did you do this thing? Why did you shed your own blood?"

Richard sobered. "So you wouldn't have to."

Arianne's heart pounded within her. If she had never cared for this man before, she now felt a deep respect and admiration for him.

"You make this sacrifice for me—to keep me from shame?" Arianne questioned.

Richard again smiled. "Too gallant, milady?"

"No," Arianne said shaking her head slowly. "Amazing—for you scarce know me and I do not love you."

"People didn't love our Lord Jesus, either, but He gave His blood to save them," Richard said, his green eyes darkening.

Still not knowing what to think, Arianne found her eyes upon his bleeding arm. Tenderly she placed her hand upon Richard. "Come," she whispered. "I will care for you."

three

The next weeks were some of the happiest Arianne had ever known. She was constantly amazed at Richard's devotion to her, all the while honoring his promise to leave her chaste.

He took time to teach her things about his home, while continuing to see to the duties that demanded his attention. She learned that he was twenty-five and held a great friendship with the King that had been firmly in place since Richard's childhood.

She also learned what had caused her father to warm so quickly to her marriage when Richard told her of a young widow who would soon be wed to her father. The arrangement would bring both wealth and property to her father. Arianne had no doubt he cared little for the huge settlement of land he'd had to sacrifice to Richard in her dowry in order to seal the arrangement. The only thing Richard ever denied her was information about his family. Whenever she questioned him concerning his parents or whether he had siblings, Richard artfully changed the subject.

They spent their days as was fitting to their station. Arianne learned the ways of the castle and found that she thrived on its running. She was quick to settle disputes between servants and relished shopping trips that allowed her to pick from among the finest furnishings to make her castle a more pleasant home.

Richard admired her abilities, and when he found her

adding figures easily in her inventory of their larder supplies, he gave her a huge purse with which to run the household in full. It eased the burden of his steward and endeared Richard to Arianne's heart.

Still, at night the old fears returned and the dread of what she did not understand. Arianne fought to sort through her confused heart and still could not tell Richard truthfully that she loved him. Until then, she felt certain that the wall of apprehension would remain firmly in place between them.

Even so, she climbed into his bed each night and curled up to the warmth he offered. He spoke softly of his days at court and his accomplishments. He shared brief details of his early childhood and asked Arianne questions that sorely strained the memories she'd buried away for so long.

"Your father seems a most difficult man. Was he always so foul tempered?" Richard questioned one night.

Arianne stiffened in his arms. "Aye." The simple word sounded painful.

Richard began to rub her arm until he felt her relax a bit. "Tell me," he whispered.

Arianne hesitantly opened her mind to the memories. Cautiously, she picked her way amidst the anguish and fear to pull out just the right words to share. "My mother never loved him and he never loved her. It was an arranged marriage to benefit their families. My mother, although she would never speak an ill word of my father, was lonely and heartbroken during her life with him. She bore him two children: my brother, Devon, and myself, and died trying to bear a third. My mother's maid told me of her death and how not even upon her final breath did my father speak any word of love to her."

"And that is why it is most important to you," Richard stated simply.

"It must be," Arianne replied as though the thought was new to her. "Yea, 'tis the reason."

Richard ran his fingers through her long wavy hair and sighed. "It is easier to understand why you hold such fear in this arrangement."

"It is?" Arianne barely whispered the question.

"You long to find the love in marriage that your mother never had. You've most carefully and completely buried your heart away to protect it from the possibility that you, too, will know the feeling of being in a loveless marriage."

"I suppose what you say is most reasonable. She died so young, yet even as she lived, my mother was a broken woman. She never knew the love of her husband, only his lust. In many ways it was most merciful that she left this earth," Arianne reasoned, "and her pain."

Richard lifted her hand to his lips and lovingly kissed each finger. "Then you will never know her pain, my sweet wife, for I already love you."

Arianne's eyes widened at his declaration. Never before had Richard mentioned love. But even as her heart told her to tread lightly, her mind reminded her of the various times Richard's actions had already spoken of his heart's true feelings.

"It is true," Richard said with a smile. "I lost my heart to you when you threw yourself at my feet and begged me to marry you."

"I did not beg," Arianne said in mock horror. "I merely insisted you keep the bargain." Her lips curled ever so slightly at the corners.

Richard laughed and held her hand to his heart. "I would never have broken that bargain," he whispered. "Nay, even if the King himself had bid me do otherwise."

Arianne could feel the rapid beat of his heart beneath her hand. Without thought, she leaned her ear to his broad chest and listened to the steady pounding.

"It beats only for you, my Arianne," Richard said, gently stroking her hair. Before long they were both asleep, but only after Richard had spent a great deal of time in silent prayer. He longed for her heart to be healed of its pain and for her fears to be cast aside. He prayed for the day Arianne would come to him without fear in her heart.

It was on these intimate nights of long, private conversation that Richard pinned his hopes. He saw Arianne warm a little more each day to his company and began taking advantage of that warming to press her a little bit further. On many occasions he'd held her hand while they strolled the grounds and in several daring moments he'd kissed her and found her very close to receptive. It became increasingly important to him that his wife come to love him.

❧

"Let us ride the estate this morning," Richard suggested after they'd shared breakfast one morning.

"I'd like that very much," Arianne answered. It had been a long time since she'd ridden.

"Good," he said, pulling her along with him. "I'd like it very much, as well." His smile was boyish and his eyes danced merrily as though they were two children stealing away from the eyes of their parents.

With Arianne secured on her sidesaddle, Richard mounted and pointed the way. "There is a path along the waterfront and I would show it to you today."

"Lead on, Your Grace," she said in a teasing tone. She often forgot to call him Richard, and at times it became quite a joke between them.

Richard pressed his horse forward and Arianne followed at a quick pace behind him until he slowed his mount and allowed the mare to catch up. They rode in silence, each enjoying the warmth of the sun and the view of the ocean that stretched out before them. They rode for over an hour before the land began to slowly slope downward toward the sea.

Arianne thrilled to the sound of the ocean upon the rocks. The power of each swell as the water pounded towards the shoreline captivated her in a way she'd not expected. It lulled her senses and she found herself forgetting all that had gone before.

Richard too, seemed to find the water refreshing. He spoke very little, occasionally pointing out some feature or fascination before leading them forward. Neither one saw the rain clouds that moved in and darkened the sky before it was too late to escape the downpour.

The rain came in torrents, saturating everything in sight. When thunder began to crack overhead, Richard sought shelter among the cliffs. "I know this land well. The cliffs will yield much in the way of protection," he reasoned with Arianne. She fought to stay seated, while each crash of thunder threatened to spill her from her saddle.

Eventually, Richard found the opening he was looking for. He dismounted and pulled the horses along a slight incline and then under the shelter of a rocky archway. Securing the horses, he reached up and pulled Arianne's drenched body from the saddle. "Come," he said above the storm and pulled Arianne farther up the cliff side.

Arianne's heavy surcoat threatened to trip her as its velvet absorbed the torrential rain. Richard finally noticed her struggles and easily lifted her into his arms and carried her to the small cave.

Once inside the shelter, Arianne realized she'd wrapped her arms tightly around Richard's neck, while burying her face against his chest. She felt most reluctant to let go and so for several moments just relished the feel of his arms around her. The storm raged outside and Arianne trembled in fear from the noise.

"You are safe, milady," Richard whispered against her ear. His warm breath caused her heart to pound harder.

Arianne forced herself to ease her hold. She felt Richard's hesitation to put her down and held her breath slightly in anticipation of what he would do.

Richard battled with his heart, mind, and soul as he held his wife. What he wanted to do was kiss her soundly and hold her. He could feel her shaking and wondered if it was the cold or her own fears which caused her to tremble. Gently he lowered her to the ground, then bid her to sit with him on the floor of the cave where he opened his arms to hold her.

Arianne didn't hesitate to move against him. She was freezing and frightened, and time had proven Richard worthy of his promise. She had nothing to fear from this man, she reminded herself and snuggled down against him.

The storm continued with no sign of letting up, and with each crash of thunder, Arianne buried her head against Richard's chest and prayed that it would soon be over.

Without thought, Richard reached down and cupped her chin in his hand, lifting her face to meet his. He felt such joy at her obvious comfort in him that he couldn't resist pressing his advantage. Slowly, with painstaking effort to keep from frightening her, Richard lowered his lips in a gentle, searching kiss. Arianne's response was accepting, prompting Richard to deepen the kiss.

When he raised his mouth from hers, Arianne's cheeks were flushed red. "My sweet Arianne," he whispered before kissing her again.

Arianne felt confused by his actions. His kisses were pleasant enough and his touch comforting, but she longed to know for sure that she loved him and as of yet, her heart could not confirm that matter. Frightened that her response might prompt a more intimate reaction, Arianne suddenly pushed away.

"I," she gasped slightly, trying to speak clearly, "I'm sorry, I can't." She started to move away, but found her gown caught beneath Richard's long legs.

"Don't be afraid, Arianne. I'll not harm you. I gave you my word. Now sit here with me and I will tell you more stories about my childhood."

Arianne immediately felt at ease. Richard had a way about him and she doubted anyone could feel uncomfortable once he sought to assuage their fears. She allowed him to pull her close once again and waited for his story to begin.

"When I was quite young," Richard told her, "I was most fortunate to foster in the care of a godly man. As was the habit of fostering, I went from my parent's home at an early age and learned how to become a man worthy of knighthood.

"This man had been to the Holy Lands and told me such tales as I could scarce believe. He told me about writings which were set upon scrolls from the time of our Lord Jesus and how they told of His life. I was determined from that moment forward to one day have a closer look at those scrolls. I set out to find a way to journey to Jerusalem."

Arianne listened in fascination at the story Richard shared.

"When my guardian learned of my desire, he took me some twenty miles to a monastery where I was allowed to study their copies of the written Scriptures. It was then that my heart was filled and my eyes opened to the truth of God. Our Lord Jesus Christ came to earth as a babe to give us life everlasting through His blood. I thought to myself, what a wonderful gift this was and the good friars of the church were amazed at my enthusiasm.

"I stayed with them for several months and studied all that they would teach. My heart craved an understanding of God, and it would not be satisfied until I had read every written Word. I spent hours in prayer, which the friars found fascinating. They naturally assumed that I would put myself into the service of the church, but it wasn't the direction I felt God's voice loudest. In fact, the church itself worried me most grievously."

Arianne sat up with a questioning look. "The church?" she questioned.

"Aye," Richard replied with a nod. "The church, it would seem, had somehow added many things that I did not see within the written Word of God. It appeared to me that man had taken upon himself to correct God's oversight."

"Your Grace!" Arianne exclaimed and crossed herself

quickly. "What heresy do you speak?"

Richard smiled, knowing that Arianne had been raised in a convent where the church's ways were stressed as divine. "'Tis no heresy I make, but a simple declaration of insight. The church would have you believe that it is the salvation of mankind, but 'tis our Lord Jesus Christ who holds that position."

"You could be hanged for heresy, or burned alive!" Arianne exclaimed with a shudder.

"I do not generally share these words with those who would see me hanged or burned," he offered with a smile. "It is only my desire to share a deep and gratifying love of our God, with you, sweet Arianne."

Arianne seemed to find reason in his words. She settled back against him and pressed a question. "Would you see the church dissolved?"

"Nay," Richard answered. "I would see it remade. I would see the Scriptures offered to all mankind and not only to a few pious priests. I would see that men and women of all rank and status would come to understand not only the fear of God as our judge, but the love of God for His children."

"It sounds quite wondrous," Arianne remarked. She realized that Richard's words of God had touched a deep chord within her. This man was nothing like her father. Duke Pemberton also saw the church as a problem, but for reasons of greed and personal gratification, not because the souls of a nation went tended without the truth.

Richard smiled at her sudden acceptance. Most would find his words beyond consideration, but Arianne actually found them worthy of contemplation.

"Have you a heart for the truth, Arianne?" Richard

questioned softly, pushing her back enough to see her face.

"Aye," she whispered, thinking not only of God's truth, but of the truth her heart might show her about Richard.

"When we return to the castle, I will show you something most precious to me," Richard stated confidently. "'Tis a copy of the Gospel of St. John. And a more wondrous book of wisdom, you will not find."

Arianne seemed surprised that Richard's personal possessions would include a rare copy of the Scriptures. "I would be most honored to view them," she said honestly. "And, perhaps you could share more about your views of God."

Richard's heart soared. He felt more confident than ever that Arianne was the proper mate for him. Now if he could only allay her fears and teach her to trust him in full.

"What of your parents?" Arianne suddenly asked. "Do they share your views on God and the church?"

Richard frowned. "Nay, they are dead." It was the first time he had spoken of them, and Arianne was taken aback by the words.

"I did not know. Has it been long?" she asked softly.

Richard shook off the question as though he'd already said too much. "Look, the storm has abated. Let's press homeward and get you dry and warm," he said pulling her to her feet. Arianne grimaced at his evasiveness, wondering again why he wouldn't speak of his family.

They stepped out of the cave and moved slowly down the slippery pathway to where the horses stood. Looking out across the sea they were rewarded with a priceless display of colors.

"A rainbow," Arianne said pointing to the sky.

"God's promise," Richard whispered against her ear.

"It always fills me with renewed hope." The previous discomfort was forgotten.

Arianne lifted her face to Richard's and wondered at the man she had married. There was so much more to Richard DuBonnet, duke of Gavenshire, than met the eye. And so many unanswered questions.

Richard, feeling her eyes upon him, dropped his gaze to the warm brown eyes which beheld him. He turned her in his arms and held her close. "Ah, sweet Arianne—my Arianne," he whispered before kissing her.

Arianne no longer battled her worries. She slipped her arms around Richard's neck and returned his kiss. The moment passed much too quickly for both of them, and when Richard pulled away, Arianne could barely make out his words.

"Much renewed hope," he whispered and helped her into the saddle.

four

Upon their return to the castle, Richard and Arianne were immediately set upon by several of the knights. Richard learned that an emissary of the King had called him to bring a good number of his men to lend protection as their entourage crossed Richard's vast open lands.

Richard brooded over the message, even while ordering his men into preparation for the trip. He didn't feel comfortable leaving the castle with so few men to defend it, but comforted himself with the thought that he had no known enemies who might lay siege to his home. Times were peaceful, and his people were content. Still, the summons did not set well with him, and his mood grew uncharacteristically harsh and somber.

Arianne too, grew somber. She knew the time would come when Richard would be called away from home, but when she learned that his absence might stretch into weeks, she became more fearful than ever. In Richard's absence, she would be in charge of the castle, and all of its problems would be hers to solve with the aid of his chamberlain and steward.

She chided herself for her misgivings, reminding herself that this was the very work she'd been trained to do most of her young life. Still, Arianne knew the task before her was a great one, and she was struggling to acquaint herself with the people whom Richard so trusted and admired.

She recognized the help she would have in Douglas and Dwayne Mont Gomeri, brothers who were Richard's highest confidants. As his chamberlain and steward, they would remain behind to offer their services to Arianne in the running of the castle and its estates.

While it was indeed rare that Richard would travel without Douglas at his side to manage his affairs, the duke felt it in the best interests of all who he loved that his chamberlain remain behind to support the new duchess. The brothers would also tend to the men left behind and the townspeople, should problems arise, but Arianne would command a place of great responsibility.

Upon reflection, Arianne was suddenly grateful to have spent so many hours in the company of Douglas and Dwayne. They dined daily with Richard and Arianne, along with several trusted knights who comprised an inner circle from which Richard drew wisdom and advice. Because of this, Arianne felt quite comfortable taking matters to them whenever Richard was unavailable.

Nevertheless, Arianne was only becoming used to Richard's presence in her life. The thought of lonely nights without his stories and shared confidences made her heart ache. She couldn't identify this new emotion. Dare she believe it was love?

It took less than a day for Richard to prepare his men, andArianne waited for the inevitable goodbye. She sat in their chamber, quietly working on her sewing and wondering when he would come to her.

Then suddenly as if answering her question, loud shouting could be heard in the hall below. Richard had been a relentless force to be reckoned with, and everyone in the household was near exhaustion in the wake of his black mood. The old apprehensions threatened to dispel Arianne's calm, and even though she felt certain that Richard's heart held love for her, she was powerless to keep the fear from her eyes. When he ranted at his men, he reminded her of her father. How could she ever convince him that she wasn't afraid, when indeed she was? Richard would never have believed her had she lied and told him otherwise, for always he said her eyes betrayed her heart.

Starting when the voices suddenly sounded in the hall-way outside her chamber, Arianne pricked her finger on the needle and had to put aside her work. She sat like a little girl, sucking on her wounded finger, when Richard blasted through the door.

"It is time," he nearly bellowed, his mind still in the mode of dealing with his men. He crossed the room with heavy-footed strides and threw open one of the clothing chests. The wooden lid banged heavily against the footboard of the bed, but Richard was oblivious.

Arianne, however, cringed at the loudness. He reminded her of her father when he shouted and banged things about. She suddenly wished she could be anywhere else but deal-ing with this raging man who would command an army to protect the King.

Richard suddenly stopped to contemplate his silent wife. As if reading her thoughts, he stepped forward to where she sat.

"You needn't fear me, milady," Richard stated firmly. "I am not your father. Now come, I would seek my plea-sure upon those sweet lips before my journey takes me far from your side." His boyish grin was all that eased the tone of his words.

Arianne sat trembling and wondered if she could even rise to her feet. "I'm sorry, Your Grace," she whispered and forgot about her sore finger. She lowered her eyes to keep Richard from seeing the tears that formed there. Were they tears of fear, frustration, or of coming loneliness?

"I've given you no reason to fear me," Richard said in complete exasperation before adding, "And stop calling me Your Grace. My name is Richard!"

"Aye," Arianne replied, jumping at his agitated voice.

"And stop jumping every time I speak, and look at me when I talk to you," Richard demanded. The dread of leaving his home had worn his patience quite thin.

Arianne raised her face to meet his. The tears in her eyes threatened to spill at any moment, and Richard's heart softened.

"I'm only a man, Arianne. Look at me. No monstrous form stands here prepared to devour you, and I haven't killed anyone in days!"

Arianne straightened a bit and looked Richard in the eye, catching the humor in his voice and the hint of a smile.

Before she could prevent it, a nervous giggle escaped her lips. Richard smiled broadly, quite pleased with himself. *At least she has a sense of humor*, he thought.

"That's better," he said. "Now come and give me a long kiss. I said I'd leave you chaste for a spell, but I did not say I wouldn't work hard to shorten that span of time."

He was her Richard again, and Arianne threw herself willingly into his open arms. "I wish you didn't have to go," she cried softly.

"You will miss me then?" he asked good-naturedly.

Arianne pulled away. "Of course, I will miss you. You are like no other man I've known. You give so much and expect so little in return."

"Oh, sweet Arianne, I expect a great deal in return," he chuckled softly. "It's just that I am a man whose patience to obtain that which he desires outweighs all else. I'm glad you will miss me, for I shan't sleep a single night without your name upon my lips and the thought of your softness upon my mind."

"Will it truly be so very long?" she questioned hesitantly. Her brown eyes framed by dark, wet lashes grew wider in fear.

"Don't be afraid. Remember, God is by your side, my sweet wife. You must leave my safety and yours in the hands of One who can better deal with it," Richard said, tracing the soft angle of her jaw. "Now, I would have that kiss."

When their lips met, Arianne wished that he might never pull away. In her heart was a sudden foreboding of separation that threatened to strangle the very breath from her. What would become of her if Richard fell to some assassin's sword?

She clung desperately to his neck, knowing that she might be hurting him in her urgency, but so uncertain of her emotions that she could not do otherwise.

Richard sensed all her worries and fears and chose the kiss instead of words to ease his wife's tormented mind. He kissed her purposefully, with a tenderness that seemed so right, so necessary, that it held Richard in awe as well. As he lingered, feeling the tension of her arms give way to trembling, he knew that Arianne cared for him, and it gave him all the drive and passion that he needed to go forth and do his King's bidding.

He pulled away, but not before her tears mingled with the sweat on his face. Would he ever dry those eyes once and for all, he wondered. So much pain was mirrored in their depths and Richard knew it was only the tiniest portion of what existed inside her heart.

"Be strong, Arianne," he whispered and gently wiped her cheeks. "Be strong and know that God is at your side. I'll be back before you know it, and all will be well."

Arianne nodded and offered the faintest hint of a smile before Richard turned away. He retrieved a bag of coins from the open chest, then without a single glance back, walked from the room and Arianne's sight.

❧

In the days that followed, Matilda was Arianne's only real comfort. She spent a good portion of each day with Arianne and often played the comforting mother that Arianne so desperately needed. Many times they took to Arianne's private solarium, the room just off her bed chamber, and spoke for hours of life at Gavenshire and Richard's childhood.

"I don't understand," Arianne said one morning. "Why won't Richard speak of his family?"

"It pains him, milady," Matilda said, offering nothing more.

"Aye, but he expects me to tell him of my woes," Arianne reasoned.

"But thou art his wife," Matilda replied. "And, he is your husband and master. If 'tis a matter for you to understand, it must be His Grace that shares the story."

"You cared for his mother," Arianne continued. "Tell me of her. Was she beautiful? Was she kind? What did she like to do? Where did she come from?"

Matilda sighed. It was from bittersweet memories that she conjured the image of Richard's mother, Lady Evelyn. "She was like a breath of spring," Matilda finally said. "She was all that nobility and gentlefolk could hope to embrace and," the hesitancy was clear in the older woman's voice, "she loved her family with a love that blinded her to all else. She saw only good in people, and because there was only good within her own heart, she presumed others were the same."

"And Richard's father?" Arianne braved the question, hoping Matilda would continue.

"Richard's father was a good man. Highly admired by the King, he was often found in his court. His death was mourned by many," Matilda responded. "'Twas his close friendship with His Highness that caused Richard to be taken under King Henry's personal care."

Arianne wanted to press for more, but something in Matilda's reply told her that they'd gone as far as the older woman would allow. "Thank you for telling me about them," Arianne whispered. "It's important that I know of them to better know my husband."

It was a start, Arianne reasoned. It was more than she'd known before, and it gave her hope that she might yet learn the full story of the people her husband kept so well hidden away.

Life moved at a painfully slow pace for Arianne. She oversaw her tasks in the castle with skill and strength born of youth, but her heart was not in it and her mind was always far from her home.

Nightly, she climbed into bed and ached for the familiar warmth of her husband. She thought for hours of how they would talk of things so seemingly trivial, yet in memory, they served to give her insight into Richard's needs and desires.

He had once told her of his love for soaking in a hot bath after working hard upon the training fields. Arianne had determined then that she would see to this need and be sure that hot water always waited in their chamber when he returned at day's end.

Then too, he'd told her of his dislikes. He despised cold food and greasy meat. He hated injustice and mock humility and found even a slightly arrogant man better than one who cowered in feigned subjection. Wool tunics chafed his neck, and he'd stubbornly clung to the same saddle for his warhorse since he'd first acquired the mount. All these things recounted themselves in Arianne's memory.

"I will line his wool tunics with silk," she mused while closing her eyes in sleep. "I will begin tomorrow, and perhaps by the time I've finished, Richard will be home." It offered slight comfort to tell herself this, but Arianne had to have something to look forward to.

❧

After nearly two weeks had passed, a messenger came to Gavenshire Castle bearing tidings from Richard. The messenger sought out the new duchess to assure her of her husband's safety and left nearly as quickly, taking back with him two of the newly lined tunics and Arianne's fondest wishes for his speedy return.

The incident had both comforted and tormented Arianne. To ease her pain, she arranged to take a long ride. Sir Dwayne accompanied her and much to Arianne's relief, seemed to understand that she didn't wish to talk.

They rode silently across the land. Only when Arianne reined her mare to a halt, high above the restless sea, did she speak. "He did not say when he would return?"

"Nay, milady, he did not," her companion replied.

"And what think ye on the matter, Sir Dwayne?"

"I cannot truly say, milady," the man spoke honestly, then added with a grin, "However, knowing how His Grace feels about his wife, I would say he will make haste in returning once the King has released him to do so."

Arianne smiled and nodded. "Richard may be a patient man, but that has never been one of my virtues. Let us return to the castle and see to the noon meal."

Sir Dwayne nodded and followed Arianne as she urged the mare into a trot. He admired this woman as he had no other, save his mother. She was intelligent and quick with solutions whenever crisis arose, but she was also kind and compassionate and he felt certain she was responsible for the happiness he'd seen in Richard's eyes. Happiness, that though haunted by an untold bitter past, seemed strong enough to dispel the ugly wounds and knit together peace and healing.

Arianne never looked back as she pushed the mare home. She'd come to love her new home, Richard's home, and for reasons beyond her comprehension, Arianne found it necessary to return quickly. Perhaps Richard had returned, she dared to hope. With that in mind she gave the mare full freedom to stretch into a jarring gallop, mindless of Sir Dwayne's surprise.

She came rapidly upon the castle and immediately spied the congregation of mounted men that stood at the gate house. "Richard has returned!" she called over her shoulder. Still she didn't slow, even though she thought her riding companion called back to her. She ran the mare the full length of the way and only reined back when she reached the men.

Arianne immediately felt a sense of confusion. She was still so unfamiliar with Richard's men that she couldn't find a single face that she could place with a name. Jumping from her horse, Arianne lost track of Sir Dwayne as she pushed through the crowd.

"Where is my husband?" she questioned one man who stood at the gate house entrance. He said nothing but pointed through the gateway.

Arianne wondered silently where Sir Dwayne was and turned to see if she could glimpse him when she walked into the solid wall of an armored man.

"Ho, wench," he said and grabbed her arm tightly. He immediately noted the richness of her garments and the ring that marked her left hand.

Arianne twisted her body to pull away from the painful grip, but found it impossible to break his hold.

"I demand that you unhand me," Arianne spat defiantly. "Sir Dwayne!" she called, but silence was her only answer.

The man who held her laughed in a low, quiet way that caused the skin on Arianne's arms to crawl. She couldn't see his face for the armor he wore, but it wouldn't matter if she could. These men were strangers, and she'd managed to place herself in the middle of them.

Lifting her chin and fixing her brown eyes on the man's covered face, Arianne was determined to show no fear.

"Who are you, and why do you handle me so?" she finally questioned.

The man suddenly released her, but Arianne knew

better than to move. She was pressed in by a dozen mounted men and Sir Dwayne was nowhere to be found. She waited silently while the man reached up to take the helmet from his head.

Hard and determined eyes stared back at her and a cruel smile played upon the lips of her captor. "You must be the Duchess of Gavenshire," he said in a tone akin to sarcasm.

"I am," Arianne replied, standing her ground. "What business have you here?"

The man looked away laughing, then in a flash turned angry eyes back to appraise Arianne. "You must satisfy the Duke greatly," he said in a guttural way that made Arianne feel sick. "I must say I am most pleased at this turn of events."

"I'm sure I do not understand," Arianne replied. She could feel her determination to be strong crumbling into the terror she'd known so much of her life. "I ask you again, what business have you here?"

Without warning, the man's mailed hand flashed out to strike her across the face. The blow sent Arianne sprawling to the ground where she sat trying to focus her eyes and rid her mind of the threatening darkness.

"You will not take that tone with me," the man sneered. "I'm not in the habit of answering for my actions to stupid women."

The words infuriated Arianne. How dare he call her stupid; but then hadn't she been just that? It was her choice to ride right up into the midst of them, offering herself over as if she were glad to see them. Slowly, she got to her feet to face the man once again. She said nothing, but her angry brown eyes spoke more than words ever could. The man actually seemed taken aback, but only for a moment.

"I will answer your question, but only because it pleases me to do so. I am here today to take you as my hostage until your husband returns so that I might seek my revenge and end his worthless life."

Arianne sank to her knees, her head still aching and ringing with the words of her husband's obvious enemy. He planned to kill Richard, and he planned to use her in order to accomplish it!

five

Arianne knew nothing except that she was being lifted up by two of the nearby men. She was half-dragged, half-carried through the gate house and into the open bailey outside the castle proper. The men who'd been left behind to defend the keep and its people drew swords and any other available weapon and stepped forward.

At the sight of the armed men, the leader raised his hand and called a halt to the thirty or so men who followed him. A half circle of Gavenshire protectors stood between the men and the castle, making their presence and intentions well-known.

The enemy leader, helmet in hand, lowered his chain mailed arm and spoke. "I am Lord Tancred," he announced. "I claim this castle for my own and its people as well. You may shed your blood here today or you may hand over your weapons in peace. Either way, you will be my prisoners until the return of your duke."

There was a murmur of voices through the crowd, but not one man offered to lower his weapons. Arianne stood proudly straight between her captors at the sight of her people. They were loyal to her and Richard and they would not bend easily.

Douglas Mont Gomeri stepped forward, sword drawn and ready to strike. He moved within ten feet of the man called Tancred, before stopping. "I am the chamberlain of this castle and in His Grace's absence, I am the protector of Her Grace and these people. We will not yield our arms to you."

"That is a pity," Tancred said and rubbed his mailed hand over his helmet, contemplating the man before him. "For you see, my foolish man, we have already captured the duchess and her guard."

At this Arianne was pushed forward to fall in the dirt at Tancred's feet. Before she could move, Tancred dropped his helmet and pulled his own sword in one fluid motion. Grabbing a handful of Arianne's hair, Tancred yanked her to her knees and held the sword to her throat. He returned his gaze to the young knight before him with an evil grin.

"Perhaps," Tancred said in a low hush, "you would like to reconsider your position."

"Nay, Sir Douglas, he knows he cannot kill me and have Richard too!" Arianne exclaimed. "He will not harm me." Arianne's self-confidence was quickly lost when Tancred's heavy hand slammed across her face. This time Arianne felt her body go limp as blackness covered her eyes.

❧

"Milady," Matilda whispered overhead. A cool cloth was brought against her face as consciousness returned to Arianne DuBonnet.

"Matilda!" Arianne gasped and struggled to sit up.

"Nay, milady. Do not move. You took quite a blow and should rest," Matilda said firmly.

"Then it is all true," Arianne stated in a resigned tone. "I had prayed it was but a nightmare, and now I awaken to find that it is cruelly true."

"I am sorry, milady." Matilda had tears in her eyes. She

rinsed the rag in the basin before applying it once again to Arianne's bruised face.

"What are we to do now, I wonder?" Arianne didn't expect Matilda to reply, but the older woman had no other choice.

"He is waiting," the maid said solemnly. "He demanded that you be brought to him the minute you regained your wits."

"What of our people?" Arianne questioned suddenly, remembering Sir Douglas' bold stand.

"They laid down their arms when he threatened to hurt you. He told Sir Douglas that he wouldn't kill you, but he would torture you until he yielded. No knight could allow such a thing to happen."

"Oh, Matilda," Arianne cried, "this is all my fault. If I hadn't put myself right in their midst, this wouldn't have happened."

"You cannot blame yourself," Matilda said softly. "No one expected this to happen. No one thought he would come."

Arianne caught a note of something in Matilda's voice. "No one thought he would come," she whispered. "Who is he?"

Just then the door slammed open and an armed man entered the room. "My master is awaiting Her Grace," he said gruffly. "I am to bring her to the great hall."

Matilda stood between the man and Arianne, trying for all she was worth to make her barely five-foot-high frame look menacing. "Milady is injured. Surely your master can wait!"

"Out of my way, woman," the man said, pushing Matilda to one side. He reached down and pulled Arianne to her feet with a snarled growl.

Arianne's head reeled from the action. She felt herself sway and might have fallen except for the strong arm that steadied her and pulled her forward.

They moved down the hall and then to the stone stairs that would take them to the floor below. Arianne looked around her as if contemplating her escape. Very little had changed except for the presence of Tancred's men. She held her hand against the side of her face where the throbbing hurt most. It caused her mind to drift unwillingly to her youth and the heavy-handedness of her father.

The man at her side seemed not to notice or to care that she was in pain. He was doing his master's bidding.

Tancred sat discussing some matter with two of his men when the knight entered the room with Arianne. The men seemed anxious to be about their orders and barely acknowledged the fact that she had joined them. Tancred noted her entrance, however, and Arianne found herself forgetting about her bruised face.

For a moment she paused, noticing that Tancred had taken the coif of chain mail from his head, giving her a better view of him. He had dark, unruly hair and piercing eyes that seemed to change color even as he lifted them in greeting. There was a lifetime of anger in the eyes that met hers, and with haughty determination, Arianne met their stare straight on.

The man at her side pushed her into a chair, where Arianne made herself straighten with as much poise and dignity as she could muster. She would not back down from this man, cowering as though she were a chambermaid. Nay! She was the Duchess of Gavenshire, and her position demanded that she act accordingly. To do otherwise would betray her people's trust.

She waited in silence for Tancred to speak, wondering who this man was and why he had come to kill Richard. If only she'd had a few more moments alone with Matilda. Matilda seemed to know exactly who he was, perhaps she even knew why he hated them so much. At the first possible opportunity, she would have to seek out Matilda and learn whatever she knew.

Tancred dismissed the man who'd accompanied Arianne, but he ignored Arianne. He leaned back against the chair she'd often seen Richard in and scowled at the wall across the room.

Arianne fought the urge to squirm uncomfortably. Perhaps that was what he wanted, she thought and doubled her efforts to remain regal and still. Finally, when Arianne thought she could take no more, Tancred turned to her.

"When is your husband to return?"

"I do not know," Arianne replied honestly. For once she was glad that she didn't know Richard's plans.

"I see," Tancred said and returned to a thoughtful mode before speaking again.

"Mayhap," Tancred began, "you think this a sport. If that is your thought, Madam, I assure you there is no game in this. I am here to take back what is rightfully mine and to avenge my name. Your husband's blood is the only thing that will do that."

"Nay!" Arianne exclaimed and jumped to her feet without thought. "You will not take him!"

Tancred laughed viciously and got to his feet. "You must love him a great deal," he replied in a sarcastic tone. Nevertheless, his words struck a chord in Arianne's heart.

"Given Richard's softness toward the lovely things of

this world, I imagine that he, too, cares greatly for you. He yearns to be home like a wounded man longs to be rid of pain. He will make his way home quickly," Tancred continued.

"My husband has already been gone a fortnight," Arianne answered. "I don't expect him to be released from his service any time soon. Why not retreat with your men before he returns? Perhaps you will be no worse for this confrontation."

Tancred snarled and stepped so close to Arianne that she could smell the sourness of his breath. "Milady, you will afford me the respect I am due. You will address me as Lord Tancred and you will serve me as master. It is my right. You are spoils of war!"

"I serve only the risen Lord and my husband," Arianne stated angrily. "I call no man Lord and will certainly not do so for the likes of you!"

Tancred slapped her, but it wasn't anywhere near the blow that had come from his mail-covered hand. "Silence, wench! You need to learn some manners."

Arianne faced him with tears stinging her eyes. She was determined to stand her ground. "Even an animal learns more from kindness than abuse," she braved.

Tancred stepped back. His expression showed his surprise at her change of tactics. Shrugging it off, he continued as though she'd never spoken. "I care not for your devotion to God or man. I have taken this castle in an act of war and by the rights of that capture, you are mine to do with as I choose. It is not my fault that your husband is a fool. He left a handful of bedraggled knights and peasants to defend a castle and keep. He must pay the price as would any other fool. He forfeits that which was once his."

"He will return," Arianne said suddenly, her heart speaking ahead of her mind. "But he is no fool to march into this castle to dance from a gibbet for your pleasure."

"Perhaps not," Tancred replied. "But I care not either way. I have you, and from what I know of your duke, he will die before he sees one hair on your head harmed."

Arianne began to tremble. "Who are you, and how is it that you know my husband?"

Tancred opened his mouth to speak, then abruptly closed it again. He went back to the table and took his seat. To Arianne, he looked completely burdened by the task before him.

"Who are you?" Arianne pressed, coming to stand on the opposite side of the table.

"It is of no concern to you."

"You plan to murder my husband and me. Do I not have a right to address my executioner?" Arianne asked.

He looked at her for a moment before a wicked grin spread across his face. "I have no plan to kill you, milady."

Arianne grimaced at the picture in her mind. "If you kill my husband and dare to lay a hand on me," Arianne barely whispered, "I will see to it myself."

"What? A devoted woman of God such as yourself, would brave the fires of hell and take her own life?" Tancred questioned with a sardonic laugh.

"Am I not already standing amidst the flames as we speak?" she inquired, pushing her hair away from her face.

"Touché, milady." For a moment Arianne saw a glimmer of something other than the hatred in Tancred's eyes. But just as quickly, the harshness returned. "It is true, you have no say in the matter. Once your husband clears my name, the King himself will demand his head and I will in turn be given these lands and your fair hand, if I so choose."

"Never!" Arianne spat the word and turned to go.

"Stay where you are! I did not give you leave."

Arianne turned. The rage in her eyes was nearly enough to silence her enemy, but the wildness of her appearance only enhanced her beauty.

"You will yield to my demands." Tancred's words were firm, leaving Arianne little doubt that he would press the issue if she did not remain silent.

"Richard will be warned," she finally said. "Someone will find a way to ride to him and warn him of your presence. My husband will not be fooled into returning empty-handed."

"He will also not be foolish enough to risk that which he no doubt prizes most," Tancred replied. "You forget, my dear Duchess. I hold his castle and folk, but most of all, I hold you. That fact alone will drive him quite mad with worry and muddy his thinking."

Arianne began to shake. She clutched her hands together tightly to keep Tancred from seeing the effect his words had. Fearfully, she realized Tancred was probably right. Richard did love her, given his patience and gentleness regarding their marriage bed. He would no doubt be determined to protect her and free her, just as Tancred said.

six

Arianne paced the confines of her bed chamber, fretting over how she might get word to Richard. The fear that Tancred would see her husband dead brought tears to her eyes and a tightness to her breast. Somehow she must save her husband!

The narrow window seemed to beckon her, and Arianne momentarily halted her pacing and went to view the situation from the opening. Nothing seemed amiss. There were men in the bailey below, some with their hauberks of chain mail clothing their bodies, others with simple leather tunics and woolen surcoats. It was really no different from when Richard's knights were in control, she thought.

People moved more quietly, Arianne noticed. Women seemed to go out of their way to keep from coming in contact with Tancred's men and Arianne was certain the reason was the men's lack of respect and chivalry. Gavenshire's people were to be treated as spoils of war, hadn't Tancred said as much? No one was safe—nor would they be until Richard was reinstated.

A light knock at her chamber door brought Arianne whirling on her heel. "Who goes there?" she called.

"'Tis I, milady," Matilda replied and Arianne quickly went to lift the bar from the door.

Arianne ushered Matilda into the room, then replaced the bar before questioning her maid. "How goes it below?"

"I cannot bear to think that His Grace will be trapped by this group of uncouth ruffians, milady. They fight amongst themselves nearly as much as they would war with our people," Matilda replied.

Arianne forgot all about asking Matilda if she knew who Tancred was and what he wanted when another knock, this one loud and demanding, struck upon her door.

"You are to take supper below with Lord Tancred," a man's gruff voice called from the other side.

Arianne rolled her eyes and Matilda openly quaked at the command. "Very well, tell Tancred I will be there shortly," Arianne replied, refusing to call the man her lord.

Matilda reached out to take hold of Arianne's arm. "You must be careful, milady. He is evil and cares not for the welfare of you or your people."

Arianne's mind was preoccupied, however, and she barely heard the words. "Help me dress, Matilda. I daren't keep him waiting."

As Matilda helped her into a clean linen tunic of pale green, Arianne's mind already raced with how she could get a messenger to Richard. "Tell me, Matilda, what have they done with Richard's men? Where are Sir Douglas and Sir Dwayne?"

"I'm afraid they've all been locked in the west tower, milady. It's heavily guarded and no one is allowed near, not even to give them food," Matilda answered and brought out a dark green samite surcoat to go over the tunic.

Arianne frowned at this news. "Someone has to ride and warn Richard," she thought aloud.

"Yes, milady, but who can go?" Matilda questioned.

She brought one of Arianne's jeweled belts and secured it around her hips before retrieving slippers from one of the chests.

"I will learn what I can while I sup with Tancred. I don't know how, but one way or another, someone will leave this castle tonight and take warning to my husband!"

Arianne walked gingerly down the stone stairway. She moved as silently as possible hoping that it might be her good fortune to overhear Tancred or his men as they discussed their plans. Her stomach growled loudly at the rich aroma of meat as it roasted on spits in the kitchen. Arianne realized she'd not eaten since morning, but with the soreness of her bruised jaw she wondered if chewing would be possible.

She entered the great hall hesitantly for all was silent except for the rustling movements of servants. It was a far cry from when Richard was in charge. With Richard, the hall was full of hungry men and others who had come at his welcome to eat. How she missed him! How she feared for him!

Moving to the table, Arianne realized that the room was not as empty as she'd hoped. Tancred sat before the fireplace, deep in thought as if contemplating the fate of the world. Her foot caught on something, making a sudden sound. Tancred sprang to his feet, hand on the hilt of his sword and eyes narrowing dangerously. Seeing it was only her, Tancred relaxed his grip and gave a mocking bow.

"Your Grace, it is good of you to honor me with your presence." His words were slightly slurred, leaving Arianne little doubt that he'd had a great deal to drink before her arrival.

She nodded but did nothing more until he held out a chair and commanded her to sit. Moving in lithe silence, Arianne did as she was bid and grimaced when he took the seat beside her.

"We will speak of your husband," he said, and then as if noticing the discoloration on her face for the first time he frowned. "You will choose your words carefully so that this is not necessary again," he said pointing to her jaw.

"'Twas not necessary the first time," Arianne stated with a fixed stare of hostility. "You are surely in command here. You are larger than me, more powerful, and you have a great many men to afford you aid should it be necessary to vanquish your foe. Surely one woman, such as myself, offers no real resistance to a great knight such as yourself."

"True," Tancred replied, motioning a servant forward. The boy placed a platter of roast before the man and started to leave. "Halt, serf!" Tancred called. "Bring more wine and be quick about it!"

Arianne watched the poor boy bow quickly before running from the room. His name was Gabe, she remembered and he had always been most congenial in his work. Funny that it should cross her mind just now. Perhaps, Arianne thought, he could be the one to get a message to Richard. It was worth considering.

When the boy returned with the wine, Tancred took it from him and poured himself a generous amount. When he reached for Arianne's goblet, she placed her hand over it.

"Nay," she spoke hesitantly. "I do not wish it."

Tancred shrugged, but Gabe paled at her protest. Arianne wished she could ease the boy's fears, but it would be necessary to ease her own before she would be of any help to others.

"I would like water, Gabe," she continued.

"Aye, milady," he replied. "I'll bring a pitcher fresh from the well." Gabe waited momentarily to receive Tancred's nod of approval.

Tancred looked first at Arianne's fixed expression and then to the boy. "Do as your lady bids," he replied and went about serving himself a huge piece of beef.

Arianne waited patiently while Tancred served himself and then, almost as an afterthought, sliced a piece of beef from his own trencher and put it on hers.

"Thank you," she replied softly.

Tancred took the acceptance of the food as a serious accomplishment and continued to fill Arianne's plate with a variety of foods after serving himself.

Gabe brought the water and Tancred dismissed him, while Arianne timidly tried to chew the meat. It was difficult, but not impossible, and her hunger was all the encouragement she needed. That and the thought that she needed to stay healthy and strong for Richard.

"You are a beautiful woman, Duchess," Tancred murmured over the rim of his goblet.

Arianne's head snapped up with a look of astonishment. What game would he play now?

As if reading her mind, Tancred reached out and snatched the head covering she wore and tossed it to the floor. Arianne's copper hair was bound in a single thick braid, which seemed to intrigue Tancred even more.

"Unbind your hair," he commanded and waited while Arianne slowly reached up to unfasten the cord that held it. She ran her fingers through the mass until the braid was unwound, then returned Tancred's stare with blazing eyes.

"Might I sup now?" she questioned with more sarcasm than she'd intended. Her tone served its purpose and broke Tancred's spell.

"By my leave," he smirked. "Eat all that you will. It will not change anything, nor will it keep you from my attentions."

"Very well, sire," Arianne replied with an over exaggerated sigh and returned her attention to the meal. She felt her hand trembling as she lifted a piece of bread to her mouth and could only pray that he did not see it. She did not wish to appear weak and vulnerable to him.

The meal continued in relative silence. From time to time, Tancred would roar out an order to Gabe for a refilling of his wine cup, but other than that he seemed content or at least tolerant to let Arianne eat in peace.

Arianne knew when she finished eating that it was a signal of sorts for Tancred to speak. She put her napkin upon the table, folded her hands in her lap, and waited for what would come.

Tancred studied her from drunken eyes. His rage toward Richard seemed muted against her beauty, and for a moment he thought of nothing but the woman beside him.

"The property of this land gives much to warm my heart," he slurred. He reached out a hand and touched the long sleeve of Arianne's tunic.

Reflexively she jerked her arm away and gasped. "Do not touch me! For all you think you own, I belong to Richard." She regretted her harsh response, fearing another strike would be her punishment, but Tancred's laughter was all that came.

"You belong to an absent duke, eh? A man who had not the wit about him to leave his lady better guarded. Nay, milady. Youbelong to me, and a more pleasant arrangement I cannot imagine."

Arianne felt her heart leap with fear. Her own safety had been far from her mind in her worries for Richard. Now a terrible thought filled her mind. What if Tancred forced himself upon her and stole her virtue before Richard and she could consummate their marriage? The thought sickened her.

"I belong to my husband," Arianne stressed. "I am his wife in the eyes of God, the church, and these people. Would you impose your will upon holy bonds?"

"I would and I do," Tancred said taking yet another deep draw of the wine.

"Is nothing holy to you then?" Arianne questioned.

"Holy? Pray tell what should I find holy, Madam?" Tancred asked, getting to his feet. He pushed the chair back abruptly, sending it backwards against the floor. He staggered back a pace, steadied himself, then glared leeringly at Arianne. "Marriage vows or naught, I made but one vow—for revenge."

"Why do you hate my husband so?"

Tancred seemed taken aback by this line of questioning. He grew thoughtful, and Arianne fervently prayed that God would somehow deliver her from the lustful hands of the man before her.

"Your husband," he spoke, twisting his lips into a cruel smile, "cost me everything that was rightfully mine. He poisoned the mind of the King and the people against me, and he must pay."

"My husband would not do that without reason,"

Arianne replied in defense of Richard. "He is a good man, kind and virtuous, and I would not hear him defamed in his own hall."

"Ugh! Good? Kind? Virtuous? Nay, milady," Tancred staggered forward and slammed his hands to the table. The very ground around her seemed to shake, and Arianne felt her heart in her throat.

Tancred moved closer to her and reached out to hold a coppery lock. "Nay, those are the words of a loving wife— a maiden in her youth besot with her husband. True love is a rare commodity in this world. Pity you waste yours on one such as Richard DuBonnet."

Tancred's words hit harder than any slap. Arianne sucked her breath in noticeably at the statement of love. Did she love Richard? Was this the proof she'd searched her heart for? Looking deep inside, Arianne felt a warmth spread throughout her body.

Yes! Arianne nearly jumped from her seat. Yes, she loved Richard! It seemed so understandably clear. Her fears for him, the way she missed him and longed for his companionship. It had nothing to do with the lust that she saw in Tancred's eyes and it had nothing to do with the fear that her mother had lived with every day of her married life. She loved Richard with a pure and free love that held no fear or contempt.

Tancred had no idea what thoughts raced through Arianne's head. He saw only the grace and beauty of the woman beside him. He longed for more than the brief touch of her silken hair.

With Arianne's thoughts on Richard, she missed the look of determination in Tancred's eyes. She was stunned when he yanked her up from her seat and tried to kiss her.

Arianne brought her foot down hard on his, but her slippers were no match for his booted feet. She pushed him away and was surprised when her small effort actually caused him to stumble backwards.

"Please, God," she prayed aloud. "Please be the protector and companion that Richard says You are and protect me from this man!" Her eyes were lifted upward for only a moment, but when she lowered them she found her prayers already answered. Tancred continued to stagger backward until he met the wall. From there, he slowly slid down until he landed with a thud on the floor.

"A waste," he murmured and passed out from the drink.

Arianne breathed a prayer of thanksgiving even as she bolted from the room and ran up the stairs.

seven

Reaching her chamber door, Arianne started at the sound of footsteps behind her. Turning, she let her breath out in a sigh of relief. "Matilda! Hurry, we must make plans."

"I feared for your safety, milady. Are you well?" Matilda hurried into the room behind Arianne.

"Aye, but not for long. 'Twas only the hand of God which kept me from sharing Tancred's bed this night. I cannot risk such a thing again. I will escape the castle and warn Richard myself," Arianne announced.

Matilda nodded. "I can help," she whispered. "Let me fetch less noticeable garments from my room. They will be a bit big for you, but with a belt they should do well enough." Arianne nodded and paced nervously during Matilda's absence.

"Dear God," she prayed, "I don't even know the land well enough to find my way, much less do I know where Richard might be. Help me, God. Please help me again."

Matilda returned breathless and thrust forward the simple garments. "These will do," she said and helped Arianne to doff her richer wardrobe.

Arianne pulled the thin linen tunic over her head. It was a dark grey color and had seen many washings. The woolen surcoat was nothing more than a shapeless shift of dark blue. She pulled it over her head and with Matilda's help tied a corded belt around her waist.

"We must hide your hair, milady, for there is no other

with such a mane. Come, I will plait in down the back and we will secure it beneath a mantel. I have a dark cloak which will hide you well in the shadows. Now, have you sturdy boots?"

Arianne nodded at Matilda's words and pointed to the chest at the far side of the room. She sat obediently while Matilda dressed her hair and then pulled the boots on while Matilda retrieved the cloak.

Peering down the hallway, the women cautiously moved toward the stairs. Matilda put her hand out and stopped Arianne suddenly. "Nay, let us use the back stairs. They lead straight into the kitchen, and from there I can get you to the tunnels below."

"The tunnels?" Arianne said in shocked, but grateful surprise.

Matilda nodded and pulled her lady along the dimly lit hall. They descended the stairs cautiously, and when they reached the kitchen, Matilda held Arianne back while she went alone to make certain the room was clear of any of Tancred's men.

"Hurry, milady," Matilda urged and pulled Arianne into the kitchen. "I will get you food and water. Stay over there in the shadows, and I will take you below in a moment." Arianne moved quickly as Matilda had instructed. It didn't matter that her servant was issuing orders. All that mattered was that she loved Richard and had to find him before he forfeited his life in Tancred's snare.

Matilda brought a small pack designed from one of the tablecloths and filled with provisions. She took one last glance around the room before slipping into the buttery where the wine was kept. Here she revealed a small trap door behind a stack of kegs. "We'll need the torch, milady," Matilda said with a slight motion of her head to the wall.

Arianne pulled the torch from its place and handed it to the woman. "I suppose this is the best way," she whispered apprehensively.

"'Tis the only way to escape unnoticed," Matilda replied and started down the ladder that would take them to the tunnels. "When I reach the bottom," she whispered back to Arianne, "throw down the pack and come quickly. Remember to pull the door shut over your head."

Arianne moved quickly and quietly and soon joined her maid in the damp, dank maze beneath the castle foundations. Matilda took hold of Arianne's arm after handing her back the pack of food, then holding the torch high, she moved down the narrow corridor. After they'd gone quite a ways, Matilda stopped for them to catch their breath.

"I must tell you how to leave this place," Matilda said after resting a moment. "We can speak freely here for no one will hear us. Richard will return from the east and so you must go in that direction once you are free of the castle. This tunnel will lead to the cliff walls over the sea. You must move down toward the beach, but not too far. You will have to work your way along the cliff wall until you reach a place where their heights are half of what they are from this place. This will be the sign you are looking for. Here you will climb upward to the top. It will not be easy, milady."

"I will manage it," Arianne stated firmly. "God will be my helper."

"Aye, that He will," Matilda replied with a weak smile. "I can see you share Richard's heart towards a merciful

God who stays at our sides."

"At first, I wasn't certain what to think about it all," Arianne mused. "Truth be told, it seemed to be heresy and I told Richard so. I had been raised to believe that the church held the only true way. But, these weeks without my husband have given me much time to consider his words. I believe that God would have us worship Him and not a religion. I might be burned at the stake for such words, but it is my heart toward the matter."

"You have a good heart, Lady Arianne," Matilda responded with such love that Arianne reflexively leaned forward and embraced the woman.

"Thank you for befriending me, Matilda. I know not what I would have done without your kindness. Now, quickly tell me what I must do after I leave the cliffs."

"There is a woods near the place where you will emerge. Take your cover there. The forest runs the length of the road for several miles and it will provide you protection from Tancred's men. The road will be the one upon which Richard will return. Rest assured that you will hear his men from the woods and you can approach him before he is endangered," Matilda answered.

"What if I move beyond the trees?" Arianne asked. "What then?"

"The land beyond the trees is hilly and open meadow land. You won't find much in the way of hiding places there. It might be best if you wait for Richard to come to you. The woods are a good ways from the castle and will give him ample time to prepare for attack. All that will matter to him is your safety. After that, he will do what he must."

"Very well. Now how do I reach the opening of this tunnel?"

"You will continue down this way," Matilda motioned with the torch. "Always stay to the right of any fork and you will soon be to the end of it." Matilda turned from Arianne for a moment and raised the torch higher. Spying what she needed, Matilda left Arianne's side and retrieved an unlit torch. Setting the second piece ablaze, Matilda handed it to Arianne. "Be certain to extinguish it before you leave the tunnel. It would be a beacon to the guards as they keep watch upon the land."

Arianne nodded, tucked the food pack down the inside of the woolen garment and took the torch. "Kneel with me, Matilda, and we will pray."

"Surely that is the very best we can do," Matilda remarked and joined Arianne on the dirt floor.

The women offered their silent prayers, then quickly got back to their feet. "God's speed, Lady Arianne."

Arianne nodded and moved quickly down the corridor. She was a woman with a mission and that mission would save the life of her husband and his men. No matter the cost to herself, she had to find Richard and warn him. Then another thought passed through her mind as she edged down the inky blackness.

"I have to tell him that I love him," Arianne breathed aloud. "Most merciful Father, let me tell him that I love him."

The tunnel soon opened out on the cliffs, just as Matilda had told her it would. It was well concealed, however, with a huge boulder that hid the opening from appearing too conspicuous. Arianne put out the torch in the soft sandy dirt and waited a moment while her eyes adjusted to the dark.

She swallowed back her fears and moved out of the

tunnel until she stood on the cliff side. Below, the water was stilled in black oblivion. Above, the moon shone dimly in a crescent sliver that would offer little light to direct her steps. Arianne moved cautiously down the rock wall as Matilda had instructed her.

It was imperative that Arianne make the forest under the cover of darkness. She would work at it all night if necessary. She felt her tender hands being torn by the sharp rocks and more than once felt her skirt catch and tear. Her courage was quickly leaving her as she drew ever closer to the water, but just then the rocks evened out and presented a path of sorts.

Arianne moved more quickly along the flattened path, but held herself back from speed, knowing that she was uncertain of each step. Hours passed before the cliff walls lowered themselves as Matilda had promised they would. Arianne gauged the heights to be half those at the castle and, summoning up the last of her determination, she began the climb to the cliff tops.

The rocks bit at her hands and knees as she inched her way upward. Silently, Arianne issued petitions to God for guidance and surefootedness, but always she kept moving—love mingled with concern motivating her forward.

At the top, Arianne stretched out her body and lay flat on the ground. She could see very little in the darkness but knew from Matilda's instructions that the shadowy blackness to her left was the woods.

After catching her breath, Arianne struggled to her feet and took off in a slow run for the trees. She slowed her step when she put her foot in a hole and nearly fell. Knowing that she could just as easily have broken a leg or twisted her ankle, Arianne tried to be more careful.

The trees loomed just ahead, and as she grew nearer, Arianne felt truly afraid. What if some wild beast awaited her in the darkness? What if she lost her way and moved in circles? She remembered Matilda's words. The forest ran along the road. She must stay close to the forest edge and keep the skies overhead in sight. When dawn came she would move further into the protection of the trees.

Keeping all of this in mind, Arianne worked for hours in the darkness. She stopped after a time, pulled the pack from her dress, and opened it. She quickly quenched her thirst and ate a piece of bread. When she started to re-wrap the contents, her hand fell upon something long and cold. Feeling it gingerly, Arianne realized it was a knife. She took it gratefully and tucked it into her belt. Now, at least, she had some form of protection.

The pack was hurriedly replaced inside her gown before Arianne moved out. Cold dampness permeated her bones, and Arianne ached from the demands of her journey. Never before had she been required to endure anything so difficult, and she was certain that had it been a mission of less importance, she would have given up.

The moon had moved far to the western skies when Arianne realized that she couldn't take another step. She managed to move deeper into the trees, knowing that she would soon collapse in exhaustion. Feeling her way in the darkness, Arianne found a clump of bushes, rolled herself beneath them, and succumbed to her body's demands. Her last waking thoughts were of Richard. Her last words were whispered prayers for his safety.

eight

Arianne came awake slowly, forgetting for a moment where she was and why. She stretched out her cramped limbs and wondered why her hands hurt so much. Then the pungent smells of dirt and decaying vegetation arrested her senses, and Arianne snapped instantly awake.

She tried to focus on her surroundings and found that she was well hidden beneath a huge mass of leafy brush. She listened, straining against the silence for any sound that would reveal a threat, either two-footed or four-legged, but nothing came.

Pushing out from her hiding place, Arianne wanted to cry aloud at the soreness of her body. She rubbed her aching legs with her cut and bruised hands before trying to stand. Finally, she felt her muscles limber some and got to her feet.

Cautiously, Arianne looked and listened in all directions. She found herself shrouded in a misty fog, yet easily recognized where the forest edge led to the road way and chided herself for not having gone further before seeking her comforts in sleep. God must truly have watched over her, Arianne mused, realizing that it wouldn't have been that difficult to spot her had a patrol been on the forest's edge.

She crept through the vegetation, trying to keep her steps noiseless. The task, however, was quickly proving impossible, as her feet crunched lightly with every move.

77

Arianne sighed and kept moving. It was the only choice she had.

After traveling for only a matter of minutes, Arianne froze at the sound of voices. She fell to her hands and knees and tried to hide herself in the underbrush of the woods.

Three men moved just outside the forest's perimeter. They were heavily armed, each sporting full chain mail hauberks and mail coifs that covered their heads. At their sides were sheathed broad swords, and mail chaussures protected their muscular legs.

Arianne's heart pounded so loudly that she was certain the men could hear its beat. She bit the back of her hand to keep from crying out in fear. Only after the men had passed and moved on a good distance did she emerge.

With Tancred's men already searching for her, Arianne doubted she would find Richard in time. She hurried, nearly running through the trees in the opposite direction of the three men. She cast a quick backward glance from beneath her hood and when she turned, ran smack into the center of a broad, chain mailed chest.

Huge arms encircled her, and Arianne realized she was caught. Fighting for all she was worth, Arianne began to kick and slap the man who held her. If Tancred thought she'd come back to him easily, he was a mistaken fool.

"What is this—a wood nymph perhaps?" The man laughed at her efforts and wrapped her tightly in her own cloak to still her actions. Arianne took advantage of the man's bare hands and lowered her teeth into the tender flesh of his thumb.

"Ahh!" the man cried out as Arianne's teeth found their mark. "You feisty vixen, I'll fix you for that." He pushed

Arianne to the forest floor, then pulled his sword and put his foot upon her shoulder to still her.

Arianne cringed back into the folds of her hood. Would he slay her here and now before Tancred had a chance to do it himself? Instead of bringing the sword upon her, the man cut into her cloak and tore a long strip from the edge. He used it as a gag which he forced around Arianne's mouth in spite of her protests. He then tore other pieces of material and bound her hands and feet. With this done, he resheathed his sword and with little effort lifted Arianne over his shoulder.

Arianne's mind was frantic. She had failed Richard in her mission and she had failed herself. Now he might never know of her love. She couldn't keep the deluge of tears from falling. As the massive bulk of a man carried her from the forest, Arianne sobbed loudly, nearly wailing by the time the soldier brought her to his camp.

The man seemed not to notice her condition. He was oblivious to her tears and Arianne was just as glad. She had no desire to evoke sympathy from her husband's enemy. Let them deal with her harshly, she thought, for it made her anger keen and her desire to fight just that much stronger.

"What have you there, George?" a man called out. Arianne couldn't see the man, but apparently he thought it great sport to tease her captor. "Seems you always did have a way with the ladies."

"This baggage is no lady," George replied and Arianne squirmed angrily at his statement. "She bit me and slapped me and would have split my skull had I handed her an axe."

The other man laughed furiously.

"Is she from the castle?" Another man questioned. This one Arianne could see from the knees down. He moved forward and lifted back her hood to reveal his helmeted face.

"Aye, she must be," George responded. "Do you know her?"

"Nay," the man replied. "But he will. Best put her in the master's tent and it will be revealed soon enough."

Arianne struggled against this news and George gave her a firm whack across her back side. "Settle it down there, wench. I've no desire to be crippled by your flailing."

Arianne ceased her struggles, but her mind raced furiously. *I must escape these men,* she thought. *I must find Richard!*

George did as he was bid and took her to a nearby tent where he dumped her unceremoniously upon a pallet. Arianne turned questioning brown eyes upward, wondering if he would untie her. She raised her hands to emphasize her stare.

"Nay," George said and shook his head. "I'll not be turning you loose upon the men. They are needed to fight the enemy and I'll not have you wounding them before battle."

Arianne struggled against her bonds and muttered beneath the gag that he was an ill-mannered oaf, but the man laughed and walked out of the tent.

With the soldier out of her sights, Arianne tried in earnest to free herself. She thought of the knife tucked inside her belt and tried to reach it, but found it was useless. She raised her hands to pull at the gag but discovered George had secured it too tightly and it wouldn't budge.

Refusing to give up, Arianne worked at the cloth until her wrists were nearly bleeding. She was tired and in pain by the time she gave in and rested from her efforts. Against her will, Arianne fell asleep and dreamed of running through the night mist to warn her beloved of a deadly enemy.

The sound of voices brought Arianne awake. She shook her head to clear her muddled mind and tried to focus on the muffled sound of men in conversation.

Her heart pounded harder as the voices grew louder.

"I assure you, sire, 'twas no small feat to bring the wench in," the voice of the one called George sounded out and Arianne cringed.

The reply was too low to give Arianne understanding, but George laughed heartily at whatever comment was made. "I'd much rather feel the taste of his steel than another bite from that sly vixen. I wish you better luck in the handling of her."

Arianne began to tremble at the words. Was she to be handed over to Tancred in this manner? Was she to meet her enemy bound and gagged without even the slightest hope of preserving her purity and life?

Dear God, she prayed, blinking back tears, *help me!*

The men were directly outside the tent, and against the shadows of early evening, Arianne could make out their movements in silhouette. The heavier of the two men was no doubt George. Arianne easily remembered that barrel-like frame. The other man still wore his helmet.

"Bring us food," the man told George. Again, Arianne struggled to make out the words that the helmet so effectively muffled. *It could be Tancred,* she thought, *but why would he risk leaving the protection of the castle?*

A mailed hand reached out to pull back the tent flap, and Arianne involuntarily sunk deeper into the folds of her cape. The man entered the tent carrying a single light which he placed on the ground opposite Arianne.

The dim glow only added to the ominous presence of the soldier. Shadows rose up from his form to make the man look like a towering sentinel. Arianne scooted away in horror, bringing his full attention to her. Pulling off his scabbard, the man gently placed his sword on the ground beside the light.

Next he reached up and pulled the helmet from his head, but Arianne still couldn't make out his features. She wasn't sure she wanted to.

The man looked down at her for a moment and Arianne found herself holding her breath. What torture would he use on her first?

The man stepped toward her. Arianne couldn't suppress a cry. She pushed back with her feet and found herself against the tent wall, unable to go any farther. His hand came down, and Arianne struggled valiantly against him. Finally, the man had both her shoulders gripped in his hands.

Arianne paused only to give him a sense of false security. Reaching to his side, he pulled out a dagger and Arianne feared she would faint. Her ragged breath came quicker and her heart raced in fear as the hand was lowered to her face. She closed her eyes tightly to squeeze out the sight of her own death.

With one quick snap the gag was broken and Arianne began to realize he did not intend to slay her. At least not yet. The man replaced the dagger and reached forward again to push back the cloak and learn the identity of his captive.

Arianne braced herself to see her captor's face, but what she saw was barely visible. The chain mail coif and the dirt smudged against his face made it impossible to tell if it was Tancred. He pushed the hood all the way off her head and gasped at the sight of her copper hair.

The roar emitted from the man was not what Arianne had expected. It was like that of a wild beast injured in a trap or a battle cry in the stillness of the night. She pushed her bound hands at the man, swinging them back and forth like a club.

"Leave me be, you cur! My husband will have your head for this!" Arianne screamed against the man's chest. She continued her tirade even as the man sought to still her.

"Cut my bonds and give me a knife. We'll see how courageous you are against an armed enemy. I won't allow you to harm my husband without killing me first. I'll warn him of your deceit, and nothing short of death will see me do otherwise!"

Arianne had no idea where her strength was coming from. The man kept hushing her, reaching out almost as if to comfort her, but Arianne knew that couldn't be possible. She felt renewed vigor when she managed to set the man off his feet. Escape was impossible, so she assailed him with praise of Richard.

"You and all the armies of the world could not defeat my husband. You may have caught us unawares, but Richard will know. He will come and cut out your heart for this!" Arianne suddenly stopped when she realized the man was laughing. The sound of his strangely familiar laughter seemed to frighten her more than his overwhelming presence had.

Turning away, his amusement lingering in the air, the man untied his coif and pulled the mail from his head. Then turning back to face her, Arianne thought her eyes were playing tricks on her.

"Richard!" she gasped and nearly fell back against the pallet.

"The very same, milady," he chuckled. "The one whom the world's armies could not defeat."

Arianne felt the realization of safety coursing through her veins. Richard reached forward and cut the bonds from her hands and feet. Shock numbed her mind, and Arianne did nothing for a moment but stare in mute surprise.

"Are you injured, Arianne?" Richard questioned, reaching out to touch her hand. He took her fingers in his mailed hand and noticed the cuts and dried blood. He frowned, feeling an anger beyond all that he'd known before.

"What other suffering have you endured?" he questioned, praying that God had been merciful to his young wife.

Dropping her hands, Richard reached for the light and brought it closer. When it shone full upon her face, Richard could see the dark bruise on her jaw. With an anguished cry, he ripped off his mail gloves and took Arianne's face in his hands.

"What has he done to you?"

nine

The agony in his voice was enough to reach through Arianne's shock. "Oh, Richard!" she cried and threw herself into her husband's arms. "I thought they'd captured me again. I thought I'd never get a chance to warn you."

Richard crushed her against his hauberk. "I feared you were dead. A rider came to warn us. The last thing he'd seen was you at the end of Tancred's sword."

Arianne kissed his face and felt the wetness there. His tears mingled with her own as she assaulted his face with kiss after kiss. "I prayed I'd find you in time," she whispered between kisses. "I had to find you and warn you. I had to tell you—"

"It doesn't matter now," Richard whispered. He was surprised at his wife's response, but knew she'd endured a great deal at the hand of his enemy.

"Yes," Arianne said and pushed away from her husband's steely chest. "Yes, it does matter. I feared I'd die before I could tell you the most important thing of all."

"Then tell me, sweet Arianne. Tell me and relieve your worried mind," he replied.

"I love you, Richard," she said and waited for his response.

Her dark eyes pierced his heart as they confirmed the words that her mouth spoke. "Are you certain?" he questioned hesitantly. "You've been through a great deal and—"

Arianne put her finger to his lips. "I love you and I desire nothing more than for you to know the depths of that love and the warmth of hope it gives me."

Richard pulled her gently into his arms and cradled her against him. For a moment there were no words he could speak. It was certainly not the ideal surrounding that he'd hoped, nay, dreamed, they'd share when she declared her love for him. But the words were just as tender, just as wondrous.

"I love you, Arianne," he whispered. "I thank God you found safety in His care and were able to bring this news to me. Still, there is an enemy upon us and I must see him defeated."

"Who is he, Richard? Why does he hate you so?"

"What did he tell you?" Richard questioned. Arianne slipped from his arms to study her husband.

"He said very little," she replied softly. "He told me he sought revenge for wrong done him by you. He told me little more than to say I was spoils of war, as was my home. He planned to use me to capture you. That was when I realized I could not send a messenger, but instead, must come to find you myself."

Richard grimaced. "Tancred is a problem from my past. One which I must rid myself of once and for all."

"Who is he and what has happened between you that such hatred cries for blood?" Arianne asked, placing her hand upon Richard's arm.

"It isn't important," he shrugged.

"Not important?" she whispered. "This man holds your home and people and you plan to end his life, but it is not important?"

Richard looked at her for a moment, then, shaking his

head, got to his feet and began to remove the hauberk. "I cannot tell you."

"I'm not a child, Richard. Why can you not tell me?" Arianne questioned more sharply than she'd intended.

"It is a thing between men," he replied in a curt tone that told Arianne the matter was closed. She refused, however, to be put off.

"Nay, Your Grace," she stated in a formal tone. "'Tis not a matter between only men. That man would have put himself in your place, not only before your people, but in my bed."

Richard whirled around, jaws clenched and eyes blazing. "You think I do not know what he is capable of?" The anger was apparent in his voice, and Arianne wished she'd not pressed the issue. Perhaps it was better that she not know the details of their war.

Richard struggled to rid himself of the chain mail, but it caught. He raged for a moment at it, before stalking from the tent without so much as a backward glance.

Tears flowed down Arianne's face and her throat ached painfully. She longed for a cool drink and something to eat, but the longing in her heart was stronger yet.

"I have driven him away," she whispered to herself. "I came here to declare my love and I have driven him from me as if he were the enemy."

She fell back against the pallet and sobbed quietly. This was not what she had hoped for.

I should never have demanded that he tell me of this thing between him and Tancred, she thought. *I should have learned from our brief time together that when Richard doesn't wish to speak of a thing, he stands firm in his resolve to remain silent.*

When her tears abated, Arianne resolved not to question Richard on any matter again. She reasoned that men often found it necessary to shield their women from the harmful, ugly things of the world. Why should she expect any different from a gentle, kind man like Richard? Hadn't he already shown her every concern?

Gathering her strength, Arianne sat up and wiped her eyes. If Richard returned, she decided, she would be nothing but the dutiful, respectful wife he deserved.

In time, Richard did return. With him came a very humble George. The man brought a tray with food and drink and placed them near Arianne. Richard, with a light-hearted voice spoke as if nothing had disturbed him from their earlier conversation.

"Sir George, I would have you meet your duchess," he said in the amused way that Arianne had come to love.

George, with a solemn look of humility bowed before Arianne. "Your Grace," he began, "I am most sorry for my behavior. I had no way of knowing that it was you. I'm most deeply regretful."

Arianne smiled and took pity on the man. "How is your thumb, George?" she asked gently.

The man raised his head with a sheepish smile. His cheeks were stained red in embarrassment. "'Tis nothing of any matter, and certainly less than what I deserved," he replied.

Arianne nodded. "'Tis well for you that my knife was out of reach, for I had full intention of slaying whatever dragon barred my way from escape."

"For certain!" Richard exclaimed. "Why, she delivered me some well placed blows while still bound from your dealings."

At this they laughed and the matter was behind them. Arianne took the opportunity to quench her thirst, while George turned to leave. At the tent flap he paused.

"I will happily guard your life with my own, milady," he spoke. "From this day forward, as long as I have breath in my body, I will see to your safety." He walked from the tent then and Arianne couldn't help but be touched by the display of chivalry.

"You have a champion, milady," Richard said, coming to sit beside her on the pallet. "I dare say, by morning's light you will find George's lance and colors firmly planted outside your tent."

Arianne smiled and reached out to touch her husband's arm. "I desire but you for my champion," she whispered.

Richard's smile warmed her, and Arianne noticed that he'd washed during his absence from her. She wished she could have done the same, knowing that she must be covered in filth.

"What are your thoughts now, madam?" Richard said, noting the change in her expression.

Arianne laughed and reached for a piece of cheese. "'Twas nothing overly endearing," she replied. "I was wishing for a bath and a clean set of clothing."

Richard chuckled. "I think we can arrange both. I was gifted by the king with many trinkets, one of which was a lovely gown for you. I will have George fetch some water while I retrieve it, but only if you promise to finish this food."

"You needn't bribe me to do that, Your Grace," Arianne stated in mock formality. "I am quite famished and only sought an excuse to keep this tray all to myself."

Richard laughed and got to his feet. "Very well. I will

see to your comforts while you gorge yourself."

An hour later, Arianne felt like a new person. She was no longer cold and hungry, nor dirty and poorly clothed. The tunic and surcoat gifted her by the king was indeed a richer garment than she'd ever worn. Pity, she thought, that it should be wasted in the middle of a fog-filled forest.

She whirled in girlish style and watched the material fall into place. The tunic was the softest blue silk, while the sleeveless surcoat was deep crimson, lavishly embroidered with gold and silver thread. Giggling in delight, Arianne hurried to finish her toilette.

Richard had even thought to find her a comb and Arianne sat untangling the waist-length bulk of copper hair, when he returned.

"You put all other women to shame," he said, coming to her side.

Arianne glanced up with her heart in her eyes. "The king was most gracious to send such a rich gift," she replied.

"I thanked him most heartily in your absence," Richard answered. "I also thanked him for arranging our marriage. I told him it was a most satisfying arrangement to me."

Arianne blushed, thinking that the arrangement surely hadn't been as satisfying as Richard would have liked. She concentrated on her hair and refused to look her husband in the eye for fear he would understand her thoughts.

"Come," Richard said and pulled Arianne abruptly to her feet. "I would show you off."

"But my hair—"

"Is beautiful just the way it is," Richard insisted.

Outside the tent, Arianne was surprised to find a small

encampment of men. Richard's tent had been set aside from the others, just far enough to afford a margin of privacy, yet close enough to defend. Arianne noticed how calm the men were. They seemed oblivious to the danger that awaited them.

When they looked up to catch sight of her, Arianne was delighted to suddenly find herself in the midst of their pampering attention. It reminded her of her wedding night when she was handed in dance from one knight to another. She learned their names and accepted their attentions, all the while noticing the gleam of pride in Richard's eyes. When Richard finally led her back to the tent, a firmly planted lance decorated the entrance flap.

"George's?" she asked, looking up to catch Richard's smile.

"Aye," he said with a nod and pushed back the canvas for Arianne to enter.

Arianne moved ahead of her husband, then turned to stop when he entered the tent. She wanted to say so much, yet words failed her. All she could do was stare at the man she'd come to love more dearly than life.

Finally, the silence grew uncomfortable and Arianne forced herself to speak. "I am sorry for the harshness between us earlier," she began. "I know there is much that I should leave to your care."

"It matters naught," Richard whispered and stepped forward to embrace his wife. "God kept you safe from harm and for that I praise Him. I know not how you escaped Gavenshire, but God must surely have directed your steps."

"He did indeed," Arianne nodded. "Matilda took me through the tunnels and then told me how to climb the cliffs and where to hide. She told me the road you would return by and then returned to the castle to face them in my absence."

"She has always served my family well," Richard remarked.

Arianne thought to question Richard further on this comment, but realizing his family was another of the subjects he desired not to speak of, Arianne instead took his hand.

With a questioning look on his face, Richard followed his wife to the pallet. The warmth of her hand in his was spreading like a fire up his arm.

"You have been most patient with me, Richard, but I would have this thing settled between us," Arianne spoke in a barely audible whisper. "I would not have another take that which belongs to you."

Richard reached out and smoothed back a copper curl from Arianne's shoulder. He thought his heart might burst from the wonder of the moment.

"I don't know what to say," he replied rather sheepishly. The moment he'd waited for since first making his vows to God and this woman, seemed somehow lost in the fog of his mind.

"Then say nothing," Arianne said, putting her arms around his neck. "It is enough that you know I love you. It is enough that I know you love me. Whatever else comes from this," she paused meeting his eyes, "is that which God intended and no man will put asunder."

Richard lowered his lips tenderly to hers and forgot about everything but the woman in his arms. Gone were the images of war and the horrors of battle. On the morrow, he would ride to meet his foe, but tonight he would find peace in the arms of his wife. Little else mattered.

ten

Arianne stretched slowly and then snuggled down into the warmth of the pallet she had shared with Richard. Images from the night passed through her mind in dreamlike wonder. How very precious the union God had given to man and woman through marriage. The love and tenderness she'd known throughout her weeks of marriage were only heightened by becoming Richard's wife in full.

Arianne thanked God silently for the love He'd bestowed upon her. Daily, it was becoming just as Richard had said: God was a personal friend to each and every one of His children. Richard had translated the Latin Scriptures to quote to her from the Gospel of St. John saying, "If anyone loves me, he will keep my word, and my Father will love him, and we will come to him, and will make our abode with him."

Arianne had pondered those words with great interest. God was offering the very best to His children. He would abide with them, not as a judge or condemner, but as a friend.

Arianne found that friendship a precious thing, and while she had been raised to respect and fear God through the church, she was only coming to know what it was to truly love and trust Him. All of this had been awakened in her spirit because of Richard.

As Arianne came fully awake, she opened her eyes and turned to study her husband. When she found the area next to her empty, she bolted upright and stared at the barren tent.

"Richard?" she whispered, knowing full well that no one would answer her.

She pulled on her clothes quickly, realizing while she did that Richard's armor and gear were gone. Without bothering to comb her hair, Arianne hurried bare-footed from the tent to find her husband.

Instead of finding Richard, Arianne found a sober-faced George and two of the men who'd been with him on patrol when he'd taken Arianne captive. All of the men seemed thoroughly embarrassed.

Arianne glanced around and saw that all signs of Richard's other men had been removed. Gone were the tents and horses. Gone were the smiling faces and the warm campfires.

"Where is my husband?" she asked George.

George stammered and refused to look her in the eye. He shifted nervously from one foot to the other, not at all in knightly fashion.

"George?" She took another step forward. "Where is Richard?"

"Gone, milady," George finally replied.

Arianne heard one of the other men's sharp intake of breath, while George seemed to take a side step, uncertain what Arianne's response would be.

"When will he return?" Arianne questioned, still not realizing the truth of the matter.

"There is no way to tell, Your Grace," George responded and quickly added, "I have food so you might break the fast. 'Tis cold, but nourishing."

Arianne managed to nod and followed to where George indicated she should sit. "Where has Richard gone that you have no inkling of when he will return? And, why did he not awaken me and bid me good day?"

George realized he would have to tell Arianne the truth. "He's gone to Gavenshire, milady. He did not wish to worry you overmuch with his departure. He bid me tell you that he will see you soon and that he—well he wanted me to say that. . ." George stammered into silence.

Arianne bit back her anger and frustration. "He wanted you to say what, George?"

"That he loves you, milady."

"Oh," Arianne replied and lowered her head. How could Richard leave her like that? Especially after all that had passed between them in the night. It was as if he couldn't trust her to have faith in him to do the right thing. But then again, hadn't she questioned him most vigorously in his dealings with Tancred?

"I'm sorry 'tis such a shock, but His Grace thought it best," George stated sympathetically.

"I'm no child to be sheltered from the truth," Arianne remarked.

"No, of course not, Your Grace," George quickly proclaimed.

"I don't wish to be treated as an addle-brained woman, either," Arianne declared, raising her darkened eyes to George.

"Never!" George stated indignantly. "Milady wounds me most grievously to declare such a possibility."

Arianne looked intently at the massive man and finally softened her glowering stare. "I apologize, Sir George. I know that you are only doing the duke's bidding. I am, well. . ." She paused, trying to come up with the right words. "I am distressed that my husband would leave without a proper goodbye."

"Mayhap it would have burdened his mind in battle," George offered without thinking.

Arianne grimaced, knowing that George was probably right. At the thought of Richard in battle, her anger faded. "Will they fight today?" She whispered the question.

George shrugged his shoulders. "'Tis a possibility, but who can say. Perhaps the enemy will give in without resistance when they see the duke's forces."

Arianne tried to reassure herself on those words, but she knew the depth of hatred between the men. She especially remembered the overwhelming desire for revenge in Tancred's voice.

"Gavenshire Castle is more than capable of keeping out unwelcome intruders," Arianne said. "Tancred will see my husband and his men as most unwelcome."

"Yea, 'tis true," George admitted. "Still, your husband has the advantage of knowing the estate more intimately. He will have a few tricks to show that man, if I know His Grace."

"Do you know this man who holds the castle? Do you have any knowledge of Tancred?" Arianne questioned.

George looked thoughtful, then shook his head. "Nay, I'm sorry, milady. In all our time at Gavenshire, I've never known your husband to have a single enemy. I'm afraid I know nothing more than I am told."

Arianne nodded her head. "It would seem we share that fate, Sir George."

They fell silent and one of the men who lingered in the background thought it a good time to bring Arianne's food and drink. She thanked him and took the offered meal, but her stomach was disinterested. Richard was in danger. How could she eat?

The day wore on in oppressive slowness. Each minute seemed to last hours and each hour was more like a day. Arianne tried in vain to learn more from Richard's men. She wanted to know how Richard would proceed once Tancred refused to open the gates to allow him entry into the castle. The men were of no help. They either wouldn't tell her or didn't know. Either way, it left Arianne more fretful than before.

She paced the small perimeter of their camp, glancing up from time to time to meet the eyes of one of her guardians. They were sympathetic eyes, but also they betrayed an eagerness to be doing something more than playing protector to their duchess. And try though they might, Richard's men could not hide their looks of worry.

Arianne finally pled a headache and retired for a rest. A fine, misty rain had started to fall and she was grateful for the shelter of the tent. Without chairs or furniture of any kind, Arianne took herself back to the pallet and stretched out.

Laying there, she could almost feel the comfort of Richard's arms around her. Why hadn't he said goodbye? At least if she could have told him—

The thought broke away from her mind. What was there that she could have said? She'd already given him the words he'd longed to hear. She'd declared her love for him. Never had any man seemed to find such contentment in a simple statement, but then Arianne knew that Richard understood the price at which her trust and love had come. No, there was nothing left for her to say, but perhaps it was more that she longed to hear reassurance from his lips. Reassurance that everything would be all right and that Tancred would soon be defeated.

"Oh, Richard." The moan escaped her lips, and tears formed in her eyes.

"Father in heaven," she prayed, knowing that no other comfort would be found, "You alone know my heart, and though I am but a mere woman, I have need to know that You are with my beloved Richard. He speaks Your name with the utmost of love and respect. His lips declare Your wonders, and praises are offered up from his heart to Your throne. Now, Father, Richard must face the enemy, perhaps to do battle with a man who would see him dead. I ask, although I am unworthy to make such a plea, that You would shroud him with protection and keep him from harm. Please deliver my husband from Tancred's hand and see this matter between them settled."

Arianne fell silent and wiped the tears from her eyes. Staring upward, she was consumed by the stillness that came to her heart. There came a peace so certain and complete that it nearly took her breath away. Clutching her hand to her breast, Arianne closed her eyes and smiled. *Yes,* she thought, *this is of God.*

❧

When Arianne awoke, she felt refreshed and at ease. Richard was still at a task that she'd give 'most anything to see avoided, but she knew for certain that God was at Richard's side.

She got up and went in search of George, who in spite of the rain and the threat of enemy soldiers, had managed to cook a rabbit over a small fire. Arianne sat with the men, trying to converse with them about the countryside and weather. She prattled on about unimportant matters, hoping to show them that her heart was confident about

Richard's fate.

It was the boredom that was setting them all on edge. As soon as the meal was cooked, one of the other men allowed the fire to die out, leaving nothing but a blackened spot where the warmth had once risen. Arianne felt the gloom of the overcast day threaten to dispel her peaceful spirit. Doubts wormed their way into her mind, but her heart held fast to a newly discovered faith in God.

She sympathized with the men as they took turns pacing the camp. With the skies growing darker and the imminent coming of night, one man was posted as guard, while the others prepared to sleep. Knowing there would be little, if any, light once the sun set, Arianne bid them good night and reclaimed the confines of her tent.

There was nothing to do but wait. Wait in the darkness, in the unbearable silence, and wonder at the outcome of her husband's campaign against Tancred.

Giving her mind over to her own curiosity, Arianne tried to remember everything she knew about Tancred. She wanted to know who this man was and why he hated her husband. It was more than a simple problem between them. Arianne knew from the look in Tancred's eyes and the tone of his voice that his conflict reached deep into his very soul. What had Richard been a part of that had caused such intense bitterness?

Matilda seemed to know who Tancred was, but Arianne hadn't been able to get her to speak in any detail. George and his companions didn't seem to understand what the conflict was about, so they were of little help. The only real understanding would come from one of two people: Tancred or Richard. And neither of them seemed inclined to tell Arianne what their war was about.

eleven

Something akin to desperation gripped Arianne's heart at the sound of scuffling and hushed whispers outside her tent.

"Who's there?" she whispered in a shaky voice.

"Milady, 'tis I, George."

Arianne tried to force her voice to steady. "What news have ye that cannot keep until the morn?"

"'Tis most urgent that we flee this place, Your Grace," George whispered from outside the tent. "The enemy is nearly upon us."

Arianne's heart pounded. The image of Tancred swam before her eyes, causing a convulsive shiver. She got quickly to her feet and rushed headlong between the tent flaps.

"Have you news of Richard?" she asked with a pleading voice.

"Nay, milady. There is no word. Take my hand and I'll lead you." He reached out in the darkness to offer his hand. Groping against the blackness, Arianne took hold of his arm. "Come, the horses are waiting."

Caring little for her own safety, Arianne allowed George to lead her through the darkness. Her mind forced images of heinous battlefields to mind. Would the blood shed there be that of her husband? *Dear God*, she prayed, *he must be safe. Keep Richard safe.*

They neared the horses, hearing their soft, nervous

snorts and hoofed pawing of the earth. Arianne didn't utter a word when George lifted her to the saddle of his mighty warhorse, coming up with the same action behind her. She knew there was no dainty sidesaddle for convention's sake. She knew too, that it would have been most uncomfortable, if not impossible, for her to ride astride in the gown she wore. Had Sir George been her love, it might have seemed daringly romantic, but George was not her love and the moment was only wrought with anxiety.

"Forgive me, milady," George whispered from behind his now secured helmet.

"Forgive you?" Arianne asked in near hushed reverence. "Forgive you for championing me and saving my frail life?" George didn't reply, but Arianne noticed that he seemed to sit a bit taller against her back.

They moved out quietly, pressing deeper into the forest in hopes of eluding the enemy. The man posted to patrol had spotted at least ten riders not far from the camp. It would be only a matter of time before they discovered the location and raided the surrounding woods.

Arianne shuddered at the thought of being once again under Tancred's control. She knew his rage and anger. What would he do after she had so completely out-foxed him? Better to pray that it did not become a possibility, Arianne surmised, for she couldn't dare to hope he would allow such a thing to go unpunished.

Rain had begun to fall again, soaking the little band as it filtered down through the trees. Arianne pitied the men who wore their mail hauberks and plated helmets. The water would make such clothing sheer misery. Arianne, herself, fared little better in the heavy, royal surcoat. Her hair, plastered down against her face, seemed more like a strangling rag than the crowing glory Richard so highly regarded. But hair would dry and so would clothing. Arianne wondered about her husband's condition. Spilled blood would not be remedied as easily as the drying of a garment.

With a heavy sigh, Arianne felt tears flood her eyes. She was quite grateful for the cover of darkness. She didn't wish to alarm her husband's men with foolish fears. Still, she knew they, too, were anxious to know the fate of their comrades.

ै

Richard DuBonnet, duke of Gavenshire, watched his castle and home from the seclusion of the nearby forest. He saw the torches that flickered boldly in the thin-slitted, first-floor windows. Windows too narrow for a man to pass through, even if they weren't barred with metal grilling. They could have been shuttered from inside the castle as well, but no doubt Tancred had put them there to mock any impending attack. He was making it clear that Richard and his men posed no real threat.

Glancing up, Richard counted a dozen or more men as they stood watch on the rampart walkway of the castle's gray stone battlements. They were unconcerned at the force Richard might bring with him. They knew full well that Gavenshire could withstand any onslaught from outside its walls.

Richard smiled to himself. What Tancred didn't expect was an assault from within. Yet, that was just what Richard planned to give him. Richard's father had once told him that a mighty castle, like a mighty man, could never be defeated from the forces outside it. With planning and prudence, both could sustain considerable exterior damage.

Yet a man and his castle were vulnerable from attacks within. A man could not ignore the attacks on spirit or heart without paying a high price. A man was almost always defeated in the realm of his mind, spirit, and heart before he gave in to an outside force. A castle was the same. If the enemy could get inside and weaken the defenses, open the doors and gates, it would only be a matter of time until the prize could be won.

Richard would divert Tancred's attentions away from the one place he would be most vulnerable. Tancred would spend so much time concentrating on the enemy outside, he would forget to keep watch from within.

Richard moved back to join his men. His mind passed quickly from thoughts of the impending battle and instead, took him back to the pleasant times he'd known with Arianne. How he loved her! Their few weeks of married life had been the foundation for a solid friendship. Their moments together the night before left Richard only more certain that God's hand wanted to bring good to both of them from the arrangement.

Richard was lighter of heart to know that he would not have to attack the castle with Arianne inside. It was hard enough to wonder how many good friends would perish in the fight without having to fear that Tancred would use Arianne as the pawn he had first intended her to be. He was greatly relieved to know she was safe in the hands of his own men, miles from harm.

&

Arianne sat rigidly straight in front of George. She ached from the position but knew she must leave George free to maneuver. She also wished that there be no appearance of impropriety to shame her or Richard. George had sworn his loyalty to guard her, but Arianne knew there was a delicate balance between her position and his. She would not be the one to create mishap between them.

Her thoughts turned once more to Richard. She worried that he might be hurt or worse. She couldn't bring herself to think that something might be horribly wrong. She couldn't bear to imagine that Tancred might have already killed him. *No,* she reassured her heart, *God is Richard's guardian. No man will come between that.*

The rain clouds moved on and allowed the slight moon to shine out overhead. Darkness had been good cover for escape, but Arianne was glad for a little light. The forest had seemed so impenetrable, so foreboding. Now she could make out the trees as they stood silhouetted against the sky. Arianne was nearly lulled into believing that they would get away unscathed, when suddenly, they were surrounded by men.

"Halt or be slain," a man cried out from behind his helmet.

"Who demands this of us?" George countered.

"I am Sir Gilbert de Meré, and I act on the orders of Lord Tancred. I have been sent to retrieve the duchess of Gavenshire and take her to his lordship."

"I will not go!" Arianne exclaimed. She would have jumped from the horse, but George's hand shot out around her.

"Nay," he whispered against her ear. Arianne froze in position. She had no idea what George would do next, but she was determined not to interfere.

"If you do not yield peaceably to us, milady," the man

spoke again, "I will be forced to kill these good men and take you anyway."

Arianne blanched and swallowed hard. She had not thought of the grave danger to Richard's men. Her men. Men who had sworn to protect and keep her with their lives.

As if reading her mind, George answered slowly. "We are pledged to guard the duchess with our lives. She is worth more than many hundred more. What are we three, that we should not give all that we possess to see her well-kept?"

"You are dead men," Sir Gilbert replied. "Even now I see your bones rotting on the floor of this forest."

"Nay!" Arianne shouted. "It will not be so!" Turning to face George, she could barely make out the glow of his eyes from behind the helmet. "I cannot allow your blood to be shed. I will go with them."

"A noble cause, indeed," Gilbert declared as he moved his horse forward.

Arianne heard the sound of swords as they were pulled from their scabbards. The ringing held a deadly tone to her ears.

"I beg you," she stated to all who would listen. "Let there be no blood shed on my account. I will go to Tancred and beg his mercy. He daren't kill me, for he would have no power over Richard."

"Will you yield, sir knight?" the man questioned.

"Nay," George replied.

Arianne put her hand out against the sword George held in his hand. "I command, as your duchess, that you lay aside your arms. Sir George, you will obey me in this." Then in a tone heard only by George, Arianne whispered, "please."

It seemed forever, before George and his companions put down their swords. Arianne knew that it went against every code of honor they had been raised with. She was surprised that her word was heeded. Perhaps George reasoned that a better opportunity would arise in which he might defeat the enemy. Perhaps he knew it was hopeless to expect victory at this time.

Gilbert de Meré moved alongside George's warhorse and pulled Arianne roughly against him. "You are prisoners of my master," he stated. "You will be taken to Gavenshire to await your fate." With that he touched his heels to the horse's flanks and moved out ahead with Arianne held tightly against him.

On the hard ride back to Gavenshire, Arianne gave thought to throwing herself from the horse. She reasoned that even if she could break the iron hold of the man who held her, the fall would most likely kill her and leave Richard with even more hatred for Tancred. No, it was better to face the future.

As the outline of the castle came into view, Arianne bit her lower lip to keep from crying. Where was Richard? Was he already within the castle or did he wait to strike? Would he see her now and grow careless in his fear for her safety?

Gilbert urged his mount forward and cried out for admittance at the castle gate house. They were quickly surrounded and escorted inside the walls. Arianne tried not to show fear. She was aware that her people watched her, and she'd not give them reason to believe she was unworthy of their trust.

The mighty oak doors of the keep opened, and with only the benefit of torch light, Arianne knew that the man in the shadows was Tancred. Gilbert halted his horse and threw Arianne to the ground.

She landed hard against her hip at Tancred's feet. Rubbing her bruised side, she dared not look up for fear he would strike her.

"Ah, Lady Arianne," Tancred said the words sarcastically. "You do me honor with your return. Come, let us speak together." He nearly growled the last few words before yanking her to her feet by her hair.

Arianne fought back tears of pain. Her rain-drenched hair made a good hold for Tancred as he dragged her into the castle.

Arianne stumbled and fell twice, but without pausing to allow her to regain her footing, Tancred hauled her up the stone stairs to the second floor.

"I should break your scrawny neck," Tancred raged as he threw her into her bed chamber. "I don't know how you escaped or who helped you, but neither matters. You were a fool to believe yourself capable of warning your husband."

Arianne paled, but remained perfectly still. Her hip was bruised to the point of distraction, yet she remained fixed to the place where Tancred had put her.

"When your husband does return, you will be the only weapon I need," Tancred said with a wicked smile. Arianne's face betrayed her fear. "But worry not, milady," Tancred said, moving to the door. "I will take you for my wife when he lies dead upon this floor."

With that he slammed the heavy chamber door behind him and Arianne heard him instruct a man to stand guard outside it. She wanted to collapse into tears, but she managed to hold them back. Getting to her feet, she moved mechanically to rid herself of the soggy garments she wore. There was no fire in the hearth, but at least she could dry off and take refuge in her bed.

"But what if he returns?" Arianne thought aloud. She hurried to don a linen tunic. *I am helpless to keep him from me,* Arianne reasoned. *I am helpless, but God is mighty and fully capable of protecting me from Tancred.*

"Father," Arianne prayed, falling on her knees and wincing at the pain in her hip, "watch over me and keep me from Tancred's plan. Protect Richard and allow him victory over this evil man. Amen."

twelve

Arianne awoke nearly a half hour before the rosy glow of dawn would grace the English countryside. There was an uncomfortable silence all around her. Throwing back the covers, she leaped from bed and ran to the window.

She looked long and hard against the early morning darkness. Something had disturbed her sleep, but what? The blackness would give up none of its secrets, and feeling that nothing else could be done, Arianne stoked up the fire in her hearth and prepared to go back to bed.

Just as the coals were stirred into life, Arianne heard a trumpeting call from outside the castle. Grabbing one of the furs from the bed, Arianne pulled it around her shoulders and returned cautiously to the window.

"I have come in the name of His Grace, the duke of Gavenshire," the man announced. "Yield the castle or meet your fate this day!"

The men on the rampart walkways laughed as though the man had said something most amusing. Looking down into the open bailey, Arianne was surprised when a small entourage of armored men appeared with torches in hand. Tancred was in their midst, barking out orders and seeing to it that each man took his post.

Tancred paused in the procession and cast an upward glance as if he knew he'd find Arianne in the window overhead. He offered her the briefest salute to let her know that he was aware of her vigil, then proceeded to the gate house.

Arianne waited for what seemed an eternity. Nothing was said and no one seemed at all eager to reply to the herald's challenge.

Finally, Tancred's voice sounded out against the silence. "Since your master is too cowardly to appear before me himself, I will address his herald and the challenge he lays forth."

Arianne held her breath. Tancred was hoping to bait Richard with the insult. Sending a herald was the commonplace thing to do and Tancred well knew it, as did the men who listened. But there was something more in Tancred's tone that made everyone take note.

"You may tell your master," Tancred called out again, "that I refuse to yield this castle. I challenge him to present himself and yield to me his titles, his land, and his people." The words chilled Arianne. She backed away from the window.

Richard's herald acknowledged Tancred's challenge and offered only one other thing. "The duke bids you take note that this castle is surrounded by some of the finest of the King's armies. The King himself demands you yield this land."

Tancred's hearty laughter was hardly what anyone had expected. "King? What King? I have no King, or has he forgotten that he exiled me from this land? You may tell your duke to come and take this castle if he can, for I will never yield what I am entitled to."

◆

Richard never heard the exchange of words that took place between his herald and Tancred. He counted on the fact that all attention would be drawn to the gate house and the surrounding walls. While the main thrust of his men, aided by many of King Henry's finest soldiers, presented a formidable force to Tancred's eye, Richard would take his most trusted and capable men through the tunnels beneath the castle. They would infiltrate Tancred's stronghold, even while he observed the forces outside the castle walls.

Halting his men, Richard raised the torch in his hand. "You know what to do. I will proceed alone, and when the appointed time comes, you will follow. The fate of Gavenshire rests on our shoulders. We will have a moment of prayer."

One by one his knights crossed themselves and knelt in the dirt of the tunnel floor. Richard knelt. "Father, we lift up our task to You. We are but humble servants and seek Your blessing to right that which has been wronged. Go with us into battle, even as you did King David of the Bible and deliver the enemy into our hands. As You will it."

The knights murmured agreements and got to their feet. Richard turned to the ladder which would allow him to infiltrate Tancred's stronghold.

"God's speed, Your Grace," the man nearest him offered. Richard nodded and took himself up.

ta

Arianne knew better than to let Tancred catch her unawares. She quickly pulled on a burgundy wool surcoat over her linen tunic, then plaited her hair and covered it with a linen headpiece.

She looked regal in her attire, but it gave Arianne little pleasure. The castle was under siege by her husband. The enemy held her hostage, and everyone's fate seemed to rest in the balance of a mysterious hatred of two noblemen. Arianne shivered, still feeling the cold in her bones. She went to a large chest and drew on a fur-lined mantel, looking much as though she were ready for an early morning walk.

The loud pounding at her door caused Arianne to take a step backward. "Unbar this door, Lady Arianne, or I shall have my men render it to kindling."

Taking a deep breath, Arianne stepped forward and removed the plank. Scarcely had she done this when Tancred burst through the door. He halted for a moment at the sight of Arianne in her stately dress. She was changed considerably from the rain-drench wretch he'd seen the night before.

Lifting her chin defiantly, Arianne met his stare. "What seek ye here?" she questioned. "Your battle awaits you below. 'Tis unseemly that you would dally your precious moments of planning in the company of a woman."

Tancred laughed in her face. "I do so appreciate a woman of high spirit. Still it is well that you learn your place. I have not yet settled with you for your disappearance from my protection."

"Protection, bah!" Arianne spat the words. "You, sire, have brought me more harm in the few moments we've shared than I've known in all the years of my life. You beat me, press your attentions upon me, and imprison me in my home. You afford me no protection, merely grief and grave reservation."

Tancred stepped forward with a leering smile. "You would surely change your mind should I relinquish my protection and turn you over to my men."

"I fear nothing that you or your men can do. I have the protection of my God and He will see you defeated this day," Arianne replied confidently.

Tancred drew back his hand and slapped her. It wasn't the fierce blow he'd dealt her before, but it was enough to bring tears to her eyes. Nevertheless, Arianne stood fast. "You seem to make it a habit of beating defenseless women."

Tancred clenched his hands into fists, uncertain how to deal with the woman who stood before him. He was used to people cowering before him, and he had certainly never met with the resistance this young woman offered. Choosing his words to break her spirit, Tancred finally answered her.

"Your cowardly husband will taste my steel this day. Bards will create songs that will tell of our battle and how I avenged my name with his blood on my sword." Tancred's eyes seemed to glow in consideration of this accomplishment.

"My husband is no coward," Arianne said softly. "If you have issue with him, why not sit down to a table and discuss it as reasonable men? Why does such hatred between you demand blood?"

Tancred seemed taken aback by her words. "'Tis no affair for a woman," he muttered.

"So I am told by both you and my husband," Arianne replied without thinking.

"So you did see him?" Tancred more stated than questioned. Arianne felt her stomach churn. What had she done?

"What know ye of his plans?" He stepped forward and grasped Arianne by the shoulders. "How does he plan to attack first?"

"I know nothing," she answered, fear edging her voice

notably.

"You lie!" Tancred exclaimed, shaking her vigorously. The rage in his eyes exploded across his face. "Tell me what he plans or I shall beat you most mercilessly."

"A dead man would find that task most difficult," a voice sounded behind Tancred, followed by the slamming of the chamber door. Both Arianne and Tancred looked up to find the armored man standing, legs slightly apart, sword drawn.

"Richard!" Arianne gasped, as Tancred whirled around pulling a dagger from his belt. He dragged Arianne across the room, distancing himself from Richard, with the knife at her throat.

"Take one step and I will cut her," Tancred said in a low menacing voice.

Richard halted, knowing the man would do just as he said. He paled at the sight of the knife at his young wife's throat. Why was she here? He had thought she'd be safely away from this matter, not plunged into the very heart of it. His calm reserve faded. The fear in Arianne's eyes blanked out all reasoning in his mind.

"Leave her be," Richard spoke in a halting voice. "Your war is with me."

"My war is with all that you hold dear. Your title, your lands, your wife. You were responsible for my losses. Now all that you possess will be mine and you will be dead."

"Nay!" Arianne cried out, struggling in spite of the dagger.

"It would seem," Tancred said, pushing the blade firmly against Arianne's throat to still her, "that your lady is quite devoted to you. Pity. No doubt, however, I will be able to change that once she is my duchess."

Richard's eyes narrowed in a hateful stare and Arianne felt her breath catch. He took a step forward, the sword still raised. "You will not kill her," Richard stated evenly. "You will not, because it would leave you defenseless."

"I did not say I would kill her, dear Richard," Tancred venomously declared. "I will, however, cause her great pain and suffering while you watch." Tancred drew the blade along Arianne's perfect face. "Scars upon such beauty would be a shame." He edged her cheek lightly with the knife, while Arianne fought to control her weak legs.

Richard could stand no more. "Do not harm her. I will give up my arms."

Arianne began to sob. "No, please don't give in to him, Richard. He will kill you."

Tancred laughed as Richard placed his sword on the floor. "It will give me great pleasure to tell the world how a woman caused your demise. Now throw down your dagger as well."

Richard did as he was instructed while Arianne continued to cry. "Move to the bed," Tancred instructed, still holding Arianne against himself.

Richard moved slowly back, while Tancred advanced until he took possession of Richard's weapons. His hand still held Arianne's arm possessively, causing Richard to grimace.

"You are a weakling, Richard," Tancred stated.

"I yielded to protect the lady's well-being. You hide behind her skirts and deny me the chance at a fair fight. I wonder now, just which of us is the weakling?" Richard's words seemed to strike their mark.

Tancred growled and pushed Arianne from him. "I've

never denied you a fair fight. You ran from it at every
opportunity, until you convinced the King to exile me.
Now I have the advantage and you cry foul."

Arianne was getting to her feet, tears blinding her eyes.
If only she hadn't been taken hostage again, Richard would
not be compromised. This was all her fault.

While the men stared at each other in silence, Arianne
considered rushing Tancred. She glanced first at Richard, then turned her attention to Tancred and back again
to her husband. As if reading her mind, Richard shook
his head.

"You needn't concern yourself, Arianne. God is with
us in righteousness and truth. Tancred knows neither and
fears not God or His people." Arianne's stare was fixed
on her husband. His words seemed to soothe her pain-
filled heart. Tancred saw the effect but said nothing while
Richard continued. "God will always deal with wicked-
ness and He will always prevail. You believe in His power,
Arianne. Never forget that God is not mocked by any man."

Arianne nodded slowly and even Tancred seemed a bit
taken aback by this declaration.

"I love you as no man has ever loved another," Richard
said with a sad, sweet smile upon his lips. "Tancred cannot change that, nor can he understand it."

"I love you, Richard," Arianne said, taking a halting
step forward. "I will give my life to preserve yours."

"Nay, love," Richard replied, shaking his head. "'Tis
not necessary."

"Enough of this," Tancred interrupted. "You will be
taken to the dungeon or cellars or tower, it matters not.
You will be held until I am able to send word to King
Henry. When I am redeemed, your life will be forfeited

and all that is yours will be mine as it was always meant to be. Including this fair child." Tancred stepped toward Arianne, but she darted away from his touch and pressed against the wall.

"I will die first," she spat at the man.

Tancred halted.

"Arianne," Richard called, and the look on his face was most grievous, "you must live. 'Tis not of God to take your life. He will preserve and keep you. Remember the way in which you came to me. God always provides a means, be it at the hand of a King or that of a maidservant."

Arianne stared in confusion at her husband. She opened her mouth to question him, as Tancred moved to the door to call his men. Richard shook his head and gave her one last smile. "Remember," he whispered.

Arianne could neither do nor say anything more. Tancred's men rushed into the room and took the willing Richard in hand. Tancred moved close enough to Richard that they were nearly eye to eye.

"Harm her and answer to God," Richard said in a whisper.

Tancred's eyes narrowed slightly. "I have never answered to God."

thirteen

Arianne opened her chamber door only enough to see that Tancred had left a man to stand guard. Silently she closed the door and began to pace the room.

"What did he mean?" Arianne whispered aloud. "What was Richard trying to say?"

She puzzled over his words throughout the day. At noon one of the servants brought her a tray of food and drink, but no one was allowed to come within, and Arianne was not allowed to venture out.

She looked out across the fields to the cliff-edged shores. Men were taking up position in a variety of places, but Arianne couldn't tell whether they were Richard's men or Tancred's. The surcoats of both armies were so similar that Arianne thought she might go mad trying to determine which was foe and which was friend.

Twice she tried to busy her hands by spinning wool on her distaff, but both times she made a matted mess and finally gave up the task. With a heavy sigh, Arianne fell back against her chair and stared up at the ceiling.

"Remember the way in which you came to me. God always provides a means, be it at the hand of a King or that of a maidservant," Richard had said. What did it mean and how could it help him now?

"I came to him through the King's edict," Arianne reasoned to the cobwebs overhead. "I came to him from my father's house. I came to him as part of a bargain, a

118

settlement of the governing powers. I. . ." Again she sighed. It was no use. Nothing made sense.

She longed to go to the castle chapel and pray. She knew Richard believed that a person could pray anywhere, at any time, and for the most part, she too, believed this was true. But the sanctuary of the chapel always made her feel closer to God. Maybe it was the extravagant stained-glass window that graced the east wall, or maybe it was the fact that there, one could shut out all other influences and turn solely to God. Whatever it was, Arianne longed for its comfort.

"Now look what you've gone and done!" a woman's shrieking voice sounded from the other side of Arianne's door.

Quickly, Arianne took herself across the room, pulling her mantel tight as though it might muffle her movement. The door creaked softly, as Arianne opened it only an inch. She studied the sight before her, unable to clearly see what was happening.

"Old crone! You nearly scalded me with that slop!" the guard raged.

Arianne opened the door a bit more and could see that the woman in the hall arguing with the guard was Matilda.

"'Twas not my fault you were born blind," she countered, noting Arianne's presence with the slightest grin on her face.

"Clean up this mess, woman!" the guard roared. "My master will not find it as humorous as you seem to. Be glad I am not given to beating women."

"Beat me?" Matilda yelled back and began screeching and crying with her eyes lifted heavenward. "Help me, oh Lord," she cried out, "for the man surely means to kill me."

Arianne knew that Matilda was staging the distraction for her benefit, but she also knew there was truth in Matilda's prayer. She hastened to ease through the chamber door and secured it behind her, all the while watching the guard as he sought to settle Matilda's ranting.

"I said I would not beat you, old crone," the man muttered over and over. "Just clean up the mess and be gone." He rolled his eyes, completely baffled by the sniveling woman who now threw herself at his feet.

"You are kind, sire," Matilda moaned her exaggerated gratitude. "Thank you for sparing my worthless life. I will do your bidding and see that this floor is cleaned. Please, I beg you, do not tell the master of this for I fear my life would be forfeited."

The man scowled, but Arianne could see from her hiding place in the shadows near the kitchen stairs that Matilda would not be harmed by the oaf.

Arianne hurried to the kitchen below, grateful that everyone moved in such hurried steps that they seemed to take little notice of one who moved with decided slowness and secrecy. She waited in the buttery, knowing that Matilda would think to look for her there.

The minutes seemed to linger, and Arianne thought more than once, she'd been discovered. But to her relief, she was safe for the moment and Matilda was soon to join her with news of Richard and the siege.

"Milady," Matilda said, embracing Arianne as though they were mother and daughter instead of servant and duchess. "I feared for your life. Is it well with ye?"

"Oh, Matilda," Arianne moaned against the older woman's shoulder, "Tancred has made Richard his prisoner and I don't know where they've taken him."

"Hush, child," Matilda soothed, "for I know of this deed as well as where they have taken your husband."

Arianne's head snapped up. "Where is he? We must free him."

"We could not do it alone, for at least two men guard him, possibly more," Matilda whispered.

"But we must help him," Arianne pleaded. "There must be a way for us to free him from his plight."

"I know of no way," Matilda said sadly. "I knew that I could detain the guard while you slipped from your room, but there would be no such distraction for the men who guard your husband. Unless you have some other thought on the matter."

"Richard was adamant that I remember something," Arianne said with a frown upon her face. "But I know naught of what he spoke."

"What did he say?"

Arianne thought for a moment. "He told me to remember the way in which I came to him. For the life of me I can't imagine what he means. I came to him by order of the King of England. What can I make of that?"

"Did he say nothing else?" Matilda asked earnestly.

"Only that God always provides a means, be it at the hand of a king or that of a maidservant," Arianne replied. "I came to Richard by the hand of the king, that much is true."

Matilda stared thoughtfully for a moment and then a smile began to line her face. "Ye also came to him by the hand of a maidservant," she whispered, "when I led you to the tunnels below."

Arianne's breath caught in her throat. "The tunnels! Richard must want me to go back to the tunnels. Where are they keeping him, Matilda? Can we get to him through the tunnels?" Arianne was already moving to the trap door.

"Nay, they've put him in the cellar. There is no passage to that place from the tunnels, but Richard gained entrance to the castle through the tunnels and he would not have traveled alone. His men must await him below, milady. Richard must desire that you tell them of his plight and take refuge there until this matter is settled."

Arianne suddenly felt hope born anew. "If Richard's men are below, they will know exactly what to do. Come help me move this door and I will go to them. We both will go!"

The women moved gingerly down the ladder, noting with satisfaction that a lighted torch offered the slightest glow from the passages below. Matilda pulled the trap door closed as she hurried to follow her mistress. She was greatly relieved to leave the conflicts overhead for the sanctuary of the tunnels.

Arianne's feet had scarcely touched the damp ground when she was surrounded by men.

"Your Grace," one of the men said coming forward. "We thought you were safely away with Sir George."

"I was captured, as were the duke's men," Arianne said and quickly added, "They have also taken my husband prisoner. He bade me find you." Another man hurried to aid Matilda down the remaining steps of the ladder.

"Where have they taken your husband, milady?"

Arianne looked around her at the eager faces. These men were Richard's most loyal or he would not have brought them with him to the tunnels. "He has been taken to the cellar and I know naught of the place, but my maid does." Arianne motioned to Matilda.

"We know of the cellars," the man replied. "We have been given tasks by His Grace. Your appearance here with this grave news gives us cause to seek them out with haste. You will remain here in the safety of the tunnels, milady, while we venture forth and see to our duties."

Arianne nodded. "Will you return and give me word of my husband?"

The man's anxious eyes scanned her face and with a slight nod, he motioned his men to the ladder. The women could do nothing but watch as the men disappeared. Fear bound their hearts with steel bands. Perhaps Tancred had learned of the trap door and even now awaited Richard's men.

Arianne shuddered and Matilda took it for chills. "Come, milady. We will seek a warmer place."

With a heavy heart, Arianne followed the older woman deeper into the maze. She couldn't help thinking of Richard and the suffering he would be enduring at Tancred's hands. *Because of me,* Arianne thought, *Richard walked right into the trap.* Just as Tancred had hoped, Arianne had been the only bait necessary to capture the young duke.

Arianne also remembered the painful expression on Richard's face as he watched and waited while Tancred put the knife to her throat.

"Why?" she exclaimed without realizing that she spoke aloud.

"Why what, milady?" Matilda asked, suddenly turning to stop.

"Why did I have to be the reason he was taken?" Her voice betrayed her emotions and broke with a sob. "Why did God allow me to be retaken by Tancred's men? I don't understand. It's only caused more suffering and now my husband is prisoner and this man will most likely seek to end his life."

Matilda grimaced and turned away from Arianne as though an unpleasant thought had come to mind.

"What is it, Matilda? What do you know that I do not?"

"'Tis nothing but speculation, Lady Arianne. I would not overburden your mind with such matters. Here," Matilda motioned, "this will be a good place to await the men."

Arianne would not be silenced with her maid's excuse. "Matilda, I must know what is going on. Do you have any knowledge of this battle between Tancred and Richard?"

"Aye, milady," Matilda replied in a weary voice. She allowed herself to sit before seeing to her lady's needs—a most unusual thing for a servant devoted to her job. "I know that the man blames the duke for lost title and lands. I know, too, that he blames Richard for King Henry's decision to exile him from England."

"But why, Matilda?" Arianne asked, taking a seat in the dirt beside her maid. "Why did the king exile Tancred?"

"That, I cannot say," Matilda replied.

"Cannot or will not?" Arianne questioned.

A rustling sound in the passageway caused both women to start. Matilda put a finger to her lips, grateful to silence the younger woman's questions. She felt a growing fear that she would have to explain to Arianne the matter of affairs between Richard and Tancred and to do so would mean to break an ancient promise to the young duke. No, she decided, she mustn't be the one to break that oath.

fourteen

The women waited in the damp darkness for what seemed an eternity. Arianne, with her questioning mind, grew restless and prayed that the time would pass quickly and allow Richard's men complete victory. Matilda, restless for her own reasons, also prayed. She prayed for a way to stay true to her promises, while providing Arianne the comfort and protection she deemed a part of her duties.

When both women were convinced that the sounds had been nothing more than rats in the passages, Matilda was the first to speak.

"Milady," she began hesitantly and in a low whisper. "It is my desire to keep a promise to the duke. It is a promise that I have held since he was a young man. This thing between him and Sir Tancred must be revealed by him alone. I cannot break my oath, no matter how much I would like to do so."

Arianne's eyes betrayed their curiosity, but she nodded in agreement. "I will not question you again," Arianne said soberly, "but only if you can assure me that in your keeping of this promise, Richard's life will not be further jeopardized."

"Nay, milady," Matilda replied. "His life will not be further jeopardized by my keeping of this oath. Both the duke and Tancred have knowledge of my understanding and what lies between them. 'Tis nothing that will cause either one to be aided or hindered."

"Very well," Arianne said, "then I must be content until my husband feels the matter is important enough to share with me. In the meantime, there is the matter of freeing Richard."

"But, milady, you heard the duke's men. We should remain here and keep safely out of sight. Richard would be most grieved if you were to be taken again and all because you sought to free him from his confines."

"That is unquestionably true," the young duchess answered. She considered the situation for only a moment before continuing. "However, I cannot sit here in the safety of the tunnels and know that he is suffering, maybe even being beaten or starved. I cannot and will not, and that is something you and my husband must understand."

"Yes, milady," Matilda said with a slight smile. "I feel the same. What have ye in mind that two women could lay their hands to?"

Arianne smiled. "I have not yet considered that matter. Perhaps if we pray on it, the heavenly Father will put it upon our minds and show us the way."

"That is most wise, milady."

Both women fell silent, and only the clasping of their hands together broke the deep concentration of their prayers. Arianne pleaded for her husband's life and freedom and begged God to show her how she might once again do something helpful to her love.

Hours passed in the silent meditation of the women, and in the end it was Arianne's concern for whether or not Richard was being fed that opened the window of opportunity for the escape plan.

"He won't be able to maintain his strength if they do not feed him," Arianne said with her hands at the side of her head. Her temples throbbed from the worry in her heart. Richard had promised her that God would win out over evil, but the moment seemed so hopeless.

"Perhaps that is our answer," Matilda said with sudden encouragement. "I can pass throughout the castle as one of the servants and no one will question my actions sbecause, of course, a servant would not be moving about without being directed by those in authority. I can go to the cellars with food for Richard and perhaps when the guards open the cellar door, he could escape."

"It has possibilities," Arianne said with a nod. "But there is too much that could happen. The guards might not allow Richard any food. They might keep it for themselves. Then, too, Richard would need a weapon against armed men, and we can't simply place one upon the tray."

"True," Matilda replied. They seemed once again to come to an impasse.

Arianne sat silently considering the situation, while Matilda got to her feet and paced the floor in front of her.

"The guards wouldn't want the food," Matilda suddenly said, "if it were nothing more than slop."

"I don't believe I understand. Richard would not desire slop, either."

Matilda smiled at the duchess and nodded. "But it would be just the kind of torment Sir Tancred would be capable of. I could tell the guards that it was all that Richard was to be allowed. If I make a stinking mess of the whole mixture, I don't believe any man would come near the tray. I have herbs and all manner of thing that can make it most unappealing. I would have to be allowed to deliver it, because the men would want no part of it."

Arianne jumped to her feet. "But perhaps they wouldn't

allow Richard to have it either."

"Of course, they would," Matilda said with her hands on her waist. "It would give them great pleasure to see Richard eating something so utterly disgusting."

"Those men being Tancred's, I suppose you are right."

"I know I am," Matilda replied confidently.

"But what of a weapon?" Arianne questioned. "Richard must have a sword or he will not be able to control the men who guard him."

"That does pose a bit of a problem," Matilda agreed.

"What if you were to hide it in your skirts?" Arianne suddenly asked. She could well imagine the possibility in her mind.

"A man's sword would extend below my limbs," Matilda said, all the while motioning to her short legs.

"A sword would be too long," Arianne acknowledged, "but a dagger or short sword could be hung from your waist, beneath your tunic. It would have to be done so in such a way that it would be easy and quick to free for use, but concealed well enough that the guards wouldn't notice."

"I think I can do that," the older woman said thoughtfully. "I could also pull a cloth around my waist like the cooks do. It would add concealment."

"Where can we get a dagger for Richard?" Arianne questioned. "We can't very well walk into the hall and ask Tancred for one."

"That is true," Matilda responded with great thoughtfulness. "Most of the men guard well their weapons, however, if I can get to one of Richard's men, I am certain he will assist us in the effort to free the duke."

"Then we must be about it," Arianne said, starting

down the tunnel.

Matilda's hand fell upon her arm. "Nay, milady. You cannot go above. 'Twould be most unwise; the men would easily recognize you."

Arianne knew that Matilda spoke truth, but she hated being left behind to do nothing. As if reading her mind, Matilda gave her a reassuring pat on the arm. "You must keep our prayerful petition before God. Knowing Richard as I do, I am certain that it is the very thing he is about, right this minute. You will stand as one in prayerful agreement before God."

Arianne immediately felt peace descend upon her troubled spirit. *Yes,* she thought, *it would be just like Richard to be quoting the scriptures he'd memorized and praying for God's guidance through his misery.*

"I will stay," Arianne agreed reluctantly. "But you must promise to return to me as soon as you can and let me know that all is well."

"I promise, milady. I will do all in my power, through His power," Matilda said pointing upward, "to free Richard from Tancred's hold."

Matilda crept through the kitchens, pulling along with her the things that she needed. She sent a whispered word here and there among trusted servants and easily concocted a hideous porridge of rotten meat and garbage.

The already potent smell was enhanced by the addition of several unknown ingredients, which Matilda cautiously threw in when no one was watching. Then, just in case Tancred's men were stupid or desperate enough to want to eat the odorous mess, Matilda added enough sleeping herbs to lay out even the heartiest soul in a long, deep sleep.

Just as she finished this task, Matilda was surprised to find one of Richard's men, Sir Bryant, dressed in the clothes of a peasant and standing at her side.

"I have the dagger you need," he whispered.

"Leave it in the buttery," Matilda replied. When she glanced up to see that the man had heard her, he was already gone.

"I will return for this in a moment," Matilda told one of the cooks. "See that no one touches it." The woman nodded and took the ladle from Matilda.

Matilda slipped through the buttery door and closed it behind her. Sir Bryant waited for her in the shadows behind several kegs of drink.

"Tell me your plan, for we must do what we can to aid in freeing our duke."

Matilda shared their plans with the young knight and waited, half expecting some rebuke or condemnation. She was gratified when none came. Instead, Sir Bryant seemed to understand that this way was best.

"I will not be far away. I will have several of Richard's best men with me and we will await word from you. Here is the weapon. Have you a way to conceal it?"

"I hadn't the chance to consider it," Matilda admitted.

Sir Bryant thought for a moment, then noticing some rope beside one of the kegs, cut off a section and came to Matilda. "This should serve the purpose. Perhaps if you tie it around your waist tight enough that the hilt will not pass through without assistance, it will remain concealed."

Matilda took the rope and motioned the young knight to afford her some privacy while she worked to secure the dagger. Once she'd let her skirts fall back into place, she asked Sir Bryant to determine her success.

"Walk to the door and back," he ordered and Matilda quickly did as he bid.

She felt the steel slide back and forth against her leg, but with a slower step, Matilda felt certain it was not perceivable, and Sir Bryant pronounced the matter settled.

Matilda moved with great slowness as she approached the passageway to the cellar. She knew that her noises would be easily distinguished in the silence of the hall, so she began an ancient sing-song tune to announce her approach.

As she came upon the guards, they were ready and waiting for her. One man advanced with his sword drawn, but then the stench of the concoction met his nose. Wrinkling his face into a grimace the man quickly stepped back.

"What have ye there, old crone? 'Tis surely nothing fit for man."

"Fit only for one man," Matilda said with a haggard laugh. "Lord Tancred," she bit her tongue to keep from taking back the title, "bid me bring this slop to the duke. He's to have naught but this for his meals."

The other man stepped forward and peered into the bowl. "What is it? It smells like death itself."

"Most probably is," Matilda played along. "Would ye care to serve him?"

Both men took a step back at this. "I won't touch that vile mixture," the first man said, while the other just shook his head.

Matilda raised an eyebrow and suddenly thought of how to buy herself more time with Richard. "I can't be leaving the bowl and tray with the prisoner. Must I take his plight upon myself and wait in that hole while he eats his fill?"

"'Twould seem your only choice," the second guard

replied. "'Tis all he's fit for anyway. The company of old women and pig's slop. Take it to him with our finest regards for his dining."

Matilda screwed up her face to show her feigned distaste with the matter, and when the men only laughed at her circumstances, Matilda knew she'd won. Now she'd have enough time to loosen thedagger and give Richard a weapon.

The men moved to the cellar door and removed the plank that held it in place. The first man called out as the second man stood ready for action.

"It seems our master is not so hard-hearted," the man spoke into the room. "Lord Tancred has sent supper to Your Grace." At that he pushed Matilda through the door and slammed it shut behind her. Only the tiniest bit of light filtered in from the slit of a single window, high in the wall.

"Your Grace? Are ye here? 'Tis Matilda." She waited a moment while her eyes adjusted to the darkness.

A sound came from her right and Matilda turned slightly with the tray in hand.

"Matilda? Why has Tancred sent you to me?" Richard asked from the darkness.

"He did not send me," Matilda whispered the reply. "Lady Arianne and I thought of this."

"Arianne? What of my wife? Is she safe? Has he hurt her again?" His voice grew louder as he neared Matilda. Then his tone changed from concern to disgust. "What is that stench?" Richard asked, coming to stand beside her.

Matilda laughed softly. "'Tis part of our plan and yes, your lady is safe."

"What plan?" Richard questioned.

"We thought to free you from your prison, sire. If you will but hold this wretched brew, I will release the weapon I've brought you from beneath my skirts."

"You managed to get a weapon in here? Did not the guards search you?" Richard asked in complete amazement.

"They would not come close enough to your supper, sire. It seems they do not have a strong stomach for such matters." She gave the tray to Richard and in spite of the dim light, Matilda turned her back to her duke and raised her skirts cautiously to free the dagger.

"Where is Arianne?" Richard whispered while waiting for Matilda to complete her task.

"She is back in the tunnels," Matilda replied, turning to hold out the dagger. "Compliments of Sir Bryant, who will be waiting just down the passageway with several of your other knights."

Matilda couldn't see his face, but she sensed Richard had a renewal of hope and strength. He took the dagger in one hand while still holding the tray in the other.

"Now what, might I ask, is your plan for getting out of here?" Richard's amusement and admiration were revealed in his tone.

Matilda took back the tray and moved toward the door. "Just follow me, Sire. I plan to douse the ambitious flames of those two pups with the stench from this tray. That should give you enough time to come through the doorway, although I'm afraid your eyes will have quite an adjustment, even in the dim light of the passageway."

"I'll manage," Richard replied. "You simply lead on."

Matilda approached the door and gave her best performance yet. "Open this door, I'll not spend another moment in here. His Grace is unreceptive to your master's gift and this stench is likely to do me harm."

Matilda and Richard both heard the rattling sound of the bar being moved. If the men were lined up as they had been when she'd entered the cellar room, Matilda would have a clear path to cover them both in the horrid concoction.

When the door opened, Matilda lost little time. She moved forward at such a pace that neither guard was prepared for the moment when she feigned a misstep and plunged the tray forward to cover them both.

"Ahhh!" the closest man cried, jumping back. The door slammed hard against the stone wall.

"Mindless crone!" the other yelled and actually dropped his sword in the attempt to rid his hauberk of the mess.

This was all the encouragement Richard needed. He rushed from the room with the dagger poised for battle, while Matilda conveniently stood with both of her feet on the discarded sword.

The entire matter took only a heartbeat and by the hand of God and the duke of Gavenshire, both men were thrown into the cellar room and Richard was free!

fifteen

"What is the meaning of this?" Tancred asked the surprised guard. They stood outside Arianne's empty bed chamber, each man as puzzled as the other.

"Mayhap there is a secret passageway," the guard offered. "A way that no one but the duke and his duchess is familiar with."

"Nay," Tancred said shaking his head. "I see no sign of that." He entered the room, however, and began to run his hand along the smooth stone wall. "Nevertheless, the wench is not here and once again she has bested me. This does not bode well with me. I will give a sizable reward to the man who finds her and brings her to me." The guard nodded and waited for dismissal. "Well?" Tancred questioned. "What are you waiting for?"

The man quickly departed the company of his sour leader. He had no desire to bear the brunt of the man's ire. It was bad enough that the woman had disappeared under his watch.

Tancred stared at the room a moment longer, then took himself to the window and looked out at the gathering of Richard's army. As the hours passed, the numbers grew. Tancred understood that Richard hoped he would be intimidated by the mass. It would seem that King Henry, feeling securely delivered to London, had spared a good many of his own men to aid Richard.

"'Tis amusing to think Henry knows I am here. He

thought to deny me my title and country, but I will show him how mistaken he was on the matter. Henry and Richard, together, haven't the power to drive me from England forever," Tancred mused.

Turning from the window he scowled at the empty room. He was quite perplexed with the young duchess Richard had taken as wife. She was no woman of tender means, of that she'd proved more than once. She was intriguing, Tancred thought, and would make him a good wife after Richard was disgraced and dead.

The sound of the herald's trumpet rang out, catching Tancred's attention. Richard was locked in the cellars, and Tancred felt it to be the proper time to relay this information to his enemy's men. Defeat would be swift without their leader.

Quickly, Tancred made his way through the castle, across the bailey, to the gate house. Along the way he noticed several of his men thoroughly searching the yards. Word must have spread quickly regarding his reward for Arianne. He smiled to himself. It would only be a matter of time and she would be under his control once again.

"What has the herald to say?" Tancred questioned the men who kept watch. His dark scowling face caused even the bravest men to step back.

"They claim the castle for the duke and bid us open the gate. If we will not yield, they are prepared to begin the assault."

"Let them," Tancred laughed. "We have their duke in the cellar below the castle. I doubt they will be so anxious to begin their assault when news of this is given."

The surrounding men joined in their leader's laughter, while Tancred took himself up to the battlements.

Many of Richard's men sat atop their mighty war horses, while others stood amassed on the ground. Their numbers were impressive, even Tancred couldn't deny this. He'd never anticipated this turn of events, having been confident that he could take Richard and the castle by surprise.

Taking a position of authority, hands on his hips and feet slightly apart, Tancred addressed the enemy. "It is well you know that I have taken the duke as my prisoner. I also have his fair wife and many of his men confined within these walls. Their execution will begin immediately if your numbers are not taken from this place."

"The duke gave us orders," one of Richard's knights said urging his horse forward a bit. "We will not disgrace him by giving up our position at the sound of your idle threats. He may well lie dead at this moment, but we will do as we were bid."

"This castle can withstand your assault," Tancred declared, yet in the back of his mind came the thought that he still had no idea how Richard had managed to gain entry through the castle walls. His men were everywhere and guards were posted all along the walkways. There was virtually no way that Richard could have made his way into the castle unseen, yet that appeared to be exactly what had happened.

Tancred's men seemed to wait for instruction, watching their leader as if puzzled about what they would do next. Tancred clenched his jaw until it ached. He couldn't very well kill Richard until he had a full confession of guilt to present to the King. Even then, it might be necessary to have Richard publicly declare his guilt, and for that reason Tancred desperately needed Arianne.

"If you attack, I will kill the duke!" Tancred declared loudly.

"He will have to catch me in order to do so," Richard called from the south wall. He was surrounded by several of his men, and in the bailey below, the sound of swords at work was already ringing out to capture Tancred's attention.

Richard's men cheered from outside the walls, while Tancred drew his sword and struck a commanding pose.

"You have but a handful of men inside the walls," he announced. "My men still outnumber yours and," Tancred said hoping that Richard was not knowledgeable of the fact that Arianne was missing, "I have your wife."

"You have nothing," Richard countered. "My wife is safely hidden. Yield to me, Tancred, and I will be merciful."

Tancred laughed. "Never! It is because of your lies to the King that I must clear my name."

Richard seemed unmoved by the words. He remained silent with a fixed stare which caused Tancred to grow uneasy. Without another word, Tancred took himself below and ordered his men to clear the bailey of Richard's soldiers.

When Tancred emerged from the gate house, Richard was gone from the rampart walkway and his men were making easy task of defeating their enemy. Motioning to several of his men, Tancred avoided the open grounds and made his way back to the castle. He had to find Arianne. She was his only hope of keeping Richard at bay.

"Has she been found?" Tancred asked the man who'd earlier guarded her chamber.

"Nay, sire," he replied. "We are sorely vexed by her disappearance, as well as the other strange happenings within these walls."

"What speak ye of?" Tancred asked.

"Half of the men cannot be found," the man answered.

"Half?"

"Well, very nearly that. I searched for my brother and our cousin, but they are nowhere to be found. When I questioned some of the other men, we totaled the numbers to equal nearly half of those who entered in with us."

"That's impossible!" Tancred declared.

"I wish it were, sire," the man said apologetically. "'Twould seem a power greater than ours stands at Richard's side."

"Bah, you prattle like a woman," Tancred said and left the man to figure out what he should do next.

Tancred moved down the shadowy corridor, fearfully watching for any sign of Richard. Should he find Richard before locating Arianne, he knew his life would be forfeited. A noise in the passage to his right caught Tancred's attention and he cautiously followed the sound.

A small woman scurried in the shelter of the dimly lit hallway. She cast a wary glance over her shoulder before hurrying down the back stairs.

Tancred followed her, immediately recognizing the woman. *Matilda!* He knew the woman well and was confident that if anyone knew where the duchess of Gavenshire had taken refuge, it would be Matilda. With a hand on his scabbard to silence any noise, Tancred moved down the stairs.

He'd barely put a foot to the bottom step when he saw the edge of Matilda's cloak disappearing around the corner. Boldly, he stepped into the kitchens, fully expecting to confront the old woman, but he was once again vexed when all he caught sight of was the overflow of her cloak as she passed from the room.

Hastening his steps, Tancred entered the buttery just as Matilda had pulled the trap door open.

"Halt!" he demanded and stepped fully into the room.

Matilda let the door drop with a resounding thud. She could only stare at the man before her.

"You were going to your duchess, were you not?" he asked, casually leaning against the wall. Matilda refused to speak and Tancred shrugged. "It is of no matter to me whether you speak or not. I know that is where you were going, and you will take me with you."

"Nay," Matilda said shaking her head. "I will not hand her over to you."

"I believe you will," Tancred said, slowly coming forward. "If you do not, I will slay you here and go below to find her. Don't be a fool, Matilda. Pull up that door and take yourself below."

Matilda moved in hesitant, jerky motions. She didn't know what else to do, fearing for her own life as well as Arianne's.

Before she could give her mind a chance to form a plan, they were in the tunnels. Tancred stared in appreciation of this discovery. "So this is how Richard gained entry into the castle," he muttered.

Matilda turned to run, but Tancred quickly caught her. "Where is she?"

"I'm not certain, sire," Matilda replied. "You know full well that the duchess has a mind of her own. She may not even be here."

"It is a chance we will take," Tancred replied, eyes narrowing slightly. "Take me to where you last saw her."

Matilda shook her head, raising her voice to protest. "I will not do it. Slay me now, but I will not betray my duke or his wife."

"Matilda!" Arianne's voice called out from down a long corridor. "Matilda, is that you?"

"Answer her," Tancred said with a sneer. "Answer your duchess." He drew his sword slowly so that it didn't make a single sound.

"Aye, milady," Matilda said. Tears came to her eyes before she let out a scream. "Run, Your Grace. Lord Tancred is here."

Arianne realized too late the trap that Tancred had set for her. She appeared not ten feet from where he stood.

Tancred saw immediately that Arianne intended to run. "Don't move or I will kill the old woman," he commanded.

Arianne froze in place. Tancred stepped forward and took Arianne in hand. Turning to Matilda, he spoke. "You will go find Duke Richard and bring him here. Tell him to come alone because if anyone, even you, shows your face in this tunnel, I will put a great misery upon this woman."

Matilda cast a glance from Arianne to Tancred and back to her duchess. Arianne knew that she awaited her approval, but how could she give it?

"I would suggest, milady," Tancred said, tightening his grip, "that you release your servant to action. Otherwise, I will be forced into a most unpleasant task."

"Go ahead, Matilda, but only as protection for yourself. Tell Richard, I will gladly give my life to spare his own. Once I am dead, Tancred will have no power over him."

Matilda hurried away, feeling much like a coward at leaving Arianne to Tancred's mercies.

When the trap door sounded in place, Arianne turned her glance to the man who held her. "At every moment I have been in your company," she began, "there is always the anger and resentment you bear upon yourself. It is almost as if it were an armor that encases you, but I perceive something else."

Tancred's expression seemed to soften. His brow raised curiously. "Pray tell, madam, what is it you perceive?"

"Pain," Arianne whispered, surprising them both.

Tancred's eyes narrowed again, but before he could speak, Arianne continued. "I see pain and emptiness. Perhaps desperation and even loneliness."

"You perceive what has never existed."

"Do I?" she asked hesitantly. The iron band of his hand upon her arm tightened.

"Aye, milady. You give me weaknesses better suited to your husband."

"My husband is a good man. He is fair and just; kind and gentle. But more than this," Arianne said, lifting her chin confidently, "he is a man whose faith is firmly rooted in God. Know ye of that peace?"

"God is for old men and addle-brained women," Tancred replied. "I have no time for a God who allows honest men to be usurped, while evil ones go unpunished."

Arianne sensed that she'd somehow struck a chord. "God's ways are often a mystery, but in time He reveals them to us."

"Through the collection plate of the church? Nay, mayhap God's revelations come through Rome and the papal displays of regality and authority. Better yet, King

Henry—there is a man after God's own heart!"

"Nay, Tancred. God need not rely upon a sovereign or a pope. It is true He uses emissaries and heralds, just as you or Richard might, but He comes to men and women as a Father and loves them."

Tancred dropped his hand as though Arianne's arm had grown white hot. "Cease this!" he ordered. "You know only what a woman's heart tells you. You can't begin to understand what a man must do."

Arianne rubbed her arm, but didn't try to move away from Tancred. She sensed that Tancred was fighting a battle of much greater proportions than his dispute with Richard.

"I might be ignorant of the affairs of men," Arianne said, her eyes gently sweeping Tancred's face, "but I believe God knows. I don't know why you were exiled or why you and my husband are at war, but God does and He is righteous. If injustice has been done, He will right it."

"But injustice hasn't been done, has it?" The voice belonged to Richard, and Tancred jumped in surprise before taking Arianne in hand once again.

"So we finally come face to face. Nothing to stand in the way. No armies, no men—" Tancred's words were cut off.

"Not face to face," Richard interrupted. "You hide behind the skirts of my wife."

sixteen

Tancred slowly, methodically offered a smile. "I do not trust you. You betrayed me to the King."

"I turned over evidence of a murderer's identity."

"You turned over false documentation and the sworn statements of my enemies!" Tancred countered.

"You forget," Richard said in a deadly tone. "I saw you myself." Arianne frowned. She struggled to understand the embittered war of words that raged around her.

"You saw nothing!" Tancred shouted.

"I saw you murder my father!" Richard cried out, stepping forward.

"Our father!" Tancred countered, pulling Arianne in front of him as a warning against Richard's advancement. "And I did not kill him!"

"Nay," Richard growled. "Never let it be said that we shared common parents."

"You are brothers!" Arianne gasped suddenly.

"Aye, but only because I cannot change the past," Richard replied bitterly.

Tancred threw his arm across Arianne and pulled her hard against him. He raised his sword to point at Richard's heart. "I came back to clear my name," he said in a low even tone. "You caused me to lose my title and lands. You took lands and wealth that should have come to me and you are responsible for sending me from my home."

"You were guilty of murder. Be grateful you were

allowed to live at all," Richard declared.

"I had no part in the murder," Tancred raged. "I told you that then and I say it again."

Richard's face darkened in a rage that Arianne had never before witnessed. Forced as she was, between the two angry men, she felt her knees weaken. Had Tancred not had a good grip on her, Arianne would have sunk to the floor.

"Father thought you a man of honor, but even after the deed is long past done, you cannot admit to your guilt and shame. Your blackened heart may cry out for revenge, but your soul is in need of absolution."

"My soul cries for justice," Tancred replied. "My soul cries for the years of loss and separation from all that I loved."

"Loved? What know ye of love?" Richard inquired venomously. "The mother who taught you love at her breast then bore your sword into her heart. What love could you have been capable of?"

"I should kill you for saying such a thing," Tancred spat. "Speak not of her again; better that we should have both died the day she perished."

The words surprised Richard and his face betrayed the fact. Arianne watched as her husband struggled with his brother's declaration.

"Were it not for Henry's mercy, you would be dead, for I desired it so," Richard finally spoke.

"The mercy of Henry?" Tancred questioned sarcastically. "Spare me words of your merciful King. The man branded me a murderer, though he had no proof. I still wear his merciful scars."

"I saw you with your hand upon the knife that had been

plunged into our father's back. Our mother was not yet dead in her own blood, two paces away," Richard replied coldly.

Arianne shuddered at the image he drew. Richard could not have been more than fifteen when he had witnessed that awful atrocity.

"I found them that way," Tancred said defensively. "I heard her screams, but I was too late."

Richard stared in disbelief at his brother. "You truly expect me to believe that?"

"Perhaps he speaks the truth," Arianne whispered. She wished she'd remained silent when Richard threw her a glaring stare. His eyes clearly silenced her, and Arianne hung her head in sorrow.

"See there!" Tancred jumped at this new opportunity. "Even your wife sees the possibility. You were so blinded by your hatred of me that you could not imagine I was telling the truth."

"And just what is the truth?" Richard's voice held no hint of interest.

"Just as I have told you. I did not kill our parents." Tancred's words were no longer venomous and Arianne sensed that the tone was nearly pleading. "I've been convinced all these years that you were the one responsible for our father and mother's death. You were conveniently there when you should have been miles away. You were the one who successfully mounted a campaign against me, in spite of your youth and inexperience, and successfully saw me stripped of my title and lands."

"You were not content with the lands you'd obtained through Henry's graciousness," Richard countered. "You wanted our father's land as well. Don't seek to ease your conscience with wild tales of my guilt. I had no hand in our parents' deaths."

"I'm past caring what explanations you might offer," Tancred said, shifting his weight nervously. "I demand that you accept responsibility for the entire matter. I demand that you send a messenger to Henry and proclaim your own guilt, for there can surely be no other who was responsible."

"You were found guilty of the crime, do you forget that?"

"I had no part in their deaths! I want my name cleared of the murders, and I want my title and lands back."

"Never!" The word reverberated throughout the tunnel.

"I will hold your sweet wife captive until the messenger returns with a full pardon. Henry, by your own admission, is quite fond of you. Perhaps he will consider that you were a wayward youth and show you mercy." Tancred's words were riddled with sarcasm. "Should King Henry refuse your admission of guilt, we will prepare a request for an audience with him in which you will openly declare, in person, my innocence and your guilt. Otherwise, I will be forced to end not only your life, but hers."

Arianne lifted her eyes to meet her husband's. Tancred brought the sword against her neck. The cold metal caused Arianne to shudder, but no more so than the look of black hatred in her husband's eyes.

"This is not her battle," Richard said slowly, never taking his eyes from Arianne. At the fear he saw there, he softened a bit. "She has endured much because of our bitterness. The least you can do is fight me man to man."

Tancred laughed bitterly. "The time for that has passed. I cannot trust you to keep your word and you will not trust me for mine."

Richard stepped back with a sigh. "What is it that you would have of me?"

"I've already told you. I want to be pardoned. I want to be reinstated in my rightful place. I want. . ." Tancred's voice fell silent for a moment. He lowered the sword from Arianne's neck. "I want to come home."

The first spark of sympathy was born in Arianne's heart for the man who held her. There was such longing in those few words.

"You will not gain your home by force, Sir Tancred," Arianne said quietly. "Nor will you find relief from the bitterness that haunts you by blaming your brother for something he did not do."

Arianne's words stunned both men. Taking advantage of their silence, she continued. "The murder of my husband will not undo the murder of your parents. King Henry is a just man. Perhaps something could be done to convince him that the charges of murder were placed upon you falsely."

"There was nothing false about them," Richard spat, causing Arianne to jump ever so slightly.

"Richard," she whispered and turned tender eyes to plead with her husband, "Tancred had no reason to risk his life and return here, if he is guilty. However, if he is innocent, no price would be too dear to pay in order to see his name cleared of such heinous charges."

"So you believe him?" Richard questioned.

Behind her, Tancred said nothing.

Arianne reached a hand out to Richard's arm, but Tancred pulled her back, fearing that Richard would snatch her away.

Arianne shook her head. "I don't know if he lies, but I do know that I would do most anything to keep him from harming you." There were tears in her eyes and Richard felt his anger fading.

"And I would do anything to keep him from harming you." Richard countered.

Tancred resented the exchange that left him feeling more alienated than before.

"Enough!" he said, pulling Arianne several feet with him. "I grow uncomfortable with this scene. Will you help me of your own free will, Richard, or must I force you?"

Richard glanced hesitantly from Arianne to Tancred. He faced his brother and for the first time honestly wondered if Tancred was telling the truth about their parents' deaths. Arianne's words gave him much to consider.

"Nay," Richard finally answered. "I cannot lie to help you. I will not admit to something I had no part in, even if you have been wrongly accused."

"Not even to save her life?" Tancred asked, nodding at Arianne.

"I cannot sin one sin to cover another," Richard replied. The pain in his face was as evident as the fear in his wife's.

"You would not tell a lie to ensure that this fair lady's life be spared?"

Richard stared deeply into Arianne's eyes, and Arianne lost her fear. God was her strength and the source of hope that she prayed for. Richard had taught her that, and because of his strong convictions, he wouldn't, nay, he couldn't, cast those beliefs aside, not even for her.

She nodded ever so slightly, telling Richard with her eyes that she understood.

"I'm sorry, Tancred," Richard spoke sincerely. "I cannot break a vow to God or tell a lie, even in order to save Arianne's life. I would gladly trade my own for hers, however, and beseech you to let her go."

Arianne watched brother confront brother, wondering which would back down first. She had no doubt that Richard was completely devoted to his faith in God. Tancred, too, was devoted, but to an entirely different cause. A cause that Arianne couldn't hope to understand.

"I can see that you are going to be most difficult to deal with." Tancred finally spoke and his words were edged with controlled anger.

"Henry would never believe that I, of my own free will, came forward to clear your name. He knows about this attack. Some of his own elite guard accompanied me to take back my castle. No matter what I say or do, Henry will know that I do only that which has been imposed upon me."

Arianne felt the heaviness of her husband's heart. The longing to free her was revealed in his eyes, and she silently prayed that God would give him direction so that the matter could be concluded without bloodshed.

"So you will not help me?" Tancred questioned slowly.

Richard shook his head. "Nay, I cannot."

"Even if it means the life of your duchess?" It was as though Tancred couldn't believe Richard would actually walk away from a chivalrous fight to defend the honor and life of one he loved.

"I did not say I would not fight for her," Richard replied, his eyes narrowing as deep furrows lined his brow. "I will give my life for hers. Let her go and face me as a man."

"I control you through her," Tancred replied, toying with the edge of the blade he held.

"Then kill her," Richard said in a cold, almost indifferent voice. "For one who declares himself incapable of murder, you certainly hide behind its threats often enough. Mercifully slay her now and be done with it."

Arianne's mouth dropped open. She stared at Richard in horror wondering what he was about. Tancred was so shocked that he pricked his finger on the blade before drawing Arianne tightly to his side.

"What's the matter?" Richard asked his brother. "Haven't ye the stomach for the task?"

"I have no desire to slay her," Tancred replied. "I am no cold-blooded killer."

"Then let her go," Richard insisted.

"Will you assure me safe passage from this place if I do?"

Richard's face contorted in anger. "Why should I?" His words were low and even as he fought to control his rage.

"I will go back into my exile," Tancred answered. "I will seek out another way to clear my name."

"You mean that you will plot my death in another manner, don't you?"

Arianne could remain silent no longer. "Please," she said lifting her eyes to meet her husband's. "Let him go and be done with this."

"He deserves to pay for the attack on my home and people. Not to mention that he has laid his hand upon you, causing great harm. Nay, he will not go free."

"But Richard," Arianne's voice was filled with pleading, "he will not give himself over. Without spilling his blood and taking his life, your brother will continue this stalemate."

"Then I will end this now," Richard said, raising his own sword.

"Nay, Richard," Arianne cried out, completely ignoring the blade that Tancred held. "His soul is not safe from the fires of eternal damnation. Would you have his blood on your head, when by mercy you could let him live to accept salvation through our Lord Jesus?" By the look on Richard's face, Arianne knew her words had hit their mark.

Tancred was at a loss to understand the battle of wills that raged inside his brother. He only knew that Richard's wife seemed desirous to save his life.

"You would be no better than those who murdered our parents," Tancred offered.

Richard looked at his brother, then sheathed his sword. "I thought you believed me the culprit of that deed."

"Nay," Tancred replied with a laugh, knowing he had the upper hand. "I never thought one so soft-hearted could be capable of using a knife for much more than threats."

Richard's hand went back to the hilt of his sword, but Arianne shook her head. "He provokes you, husband. Be not concerned with his tongue, but remember his soul."

Richard was amazed at Arianne's calm. She had learned so well his love of God and desire that all mankind would come to be saved that there was no doubt who would win this hand.

Tancred, too, sensed the control Arianne's words had upon her husband. What troubled him was the effect those soft-spoken words had upon his own heart and mind. He had to distance himself from her gentle concern. There was no room for it in this fight.

"Will you let me rejoin my ship?" Tancred finally asked. Richard stepped back a pace. "Aye."

"And you will give me your oath on the Code of Nobles that you will do nothing to hinder me from passing from your estates?"

"I give you my word. You may leave to return to your exile," Richard promised. "Release Arianne and I will guide you through the tunnels to your ship."

Tancred shook his head, not trusting his brother. "Nay, Arianne knows the way, for obviously this is the means by which she escaped me before. She will guide me to the ship so that no harm will befall me."

Richard's clenched fists were clear signs of his displeasure, but before he could open his mouth, Arianne lifted her hand.

"I will show him the way, Richard. God will not see me suffer at his hands anymore. Put into practice that faith which so strengthens those around you." Her words were peaceful balm on the wounds of Richard's heart. God was in charge of the matter, as Arianne so simply had reminded him.

It went against everything he'd ever known, but Richard backed away and, making a sweeping bow, gave his brother what he demanded. "Arianne will lead you. I will arrange for your men to be at the ship, but mark my words, dear brother, my men will be there also." Then almost as an afterthought, Richard added, "As will I."

Tancred offered his brother a mocking salute. "I will see you at the ship then."

Richard nodded and met Arianne's eyes. "I will come for you, my sweet Arianne. Fear naught, for God is your protector and keeper."

Arianne nodded, feeling complete peace in the matter. God would see her through this, and nothing Tancred could do or say would change how fully she had come to understand her heavenly Father's power. God was in control of the matter, she reasoned. Therefore, Tancred had no power over her life.

"Come along," Arianne bid Tancred. If they didn't move out, she feared, Richard might change his mind.

seventeen

The harsh dampness of the tunnels made Arianne shiver. She longed to pull the torch closer to her body for warmth, but Tancred seemed unconcerned with her plight and hurried her forward.

Nearing the tunnel opening, Arianne could hear the crashing waves on the rocks below like a great churning caldron. She wondered if the beach would be covered and if they would have to climb the rocks. Silently, she offered a prayer for strength, knowing that of her own accord she could never make it.

"We are nearly outside," Arianne whispered to the man beside her.

"Aye, I hear the sea," replied Tancred.

"It must be difficult to leave again."

"I beg your pardon?"

Arianne swallowed hard. Had she the bravery to continue this conversation? "I was only saying that it must be painful to leave your home again."

"Gavenshire is not my home. It was awarded to my brother after his faithful service to Henry. My lands were well to the south," Tancred replied with uncharacteristic softness.

"Does my husband also control those?"

"Nay, he didn't want them, so Henry took them," Tancred answered. Light from the tunnel opening guided their steps. "Hurry thy pace that we may reach my ship before Richard."

"Richard will have little trouble getting there ahead of us," Arianne replied. "We still have to climb down to the beach, or if the water is too high, we must climb up the cliff side. 'Twill be no easy matter for me, I assure you."

"You'll have plenty of time to rest once we're aboard my ship."

Arianne stopped dead in her tracks. Tancred was quite serious. "You mean to take me after giving Richard your word that you would leave me unharmed?"

"I don't intend to harm you," Tancred replied softly. He looked at Arianne with new eyes. "I am most sorry for the way I've treated you in the past, but it was necessary to take control. You must believe me. I will see my name cleared, and I will use whatever means I must in order to do just that."

"But you cannot hope to take me!" exclaimed Arianne. "Richard will never allow it."

"My brother loves you more than life," Tancred said, putting out the torch in the sandy soil of the tunnel floor. "I can count on that."

Arianne said nothing more. Tancred pulled her out into the sunlight and surveyed the scene.

"There is adequate clearance for us to take to the shore. We will be quick enough, and my ship is no more than a half a league around the bend. Come along, milady."

Arianne's mind mulled over Tancred's plan even as he assisted her down the rocky path. She was amazed at the change in his attitude toward her. Perhaps the words she'd spoken had made him think about his plight. Perhaps no one had ever cared to defend him before.

"Sir Tancred," Arianne said, fighting with the skirt of

her gown, "I do not fear you any longer."

The words seemed a bold declaration under the circumstances, but Tancred was not offended. He glanced over his shoulder at her with a smile so similar to Richard's that Arianne was stunned.

"It is well that you do not," Tancred replied. "I have no need for more enemies. I perceive that you see something of value in this exiled hide of mine. I do, however, require that you replace what once was fear with a healthy respect for my will. I am not a puppet to be played with, milady, and in spite of my brother's pliability, you will not find me a character to be dallied with."

"You have much to overcome, sire," Arianne replied thoughtfully. "I must believe that you were reared to fear God, as Richard was. I must further believe from the stories my husband has told that you, too, must have listened to stories at your mother's knee."

"Speak not of my mother," Tancred said in a warning tone. "I will not hear of it."

"She must have loved you greatly," Arianne dared to continue. "I have heard Matilda speak of her."

"Enough!" Tancred said harshly and yanked Arianne's arm.

Arianne remained silent while they worked their way down to the beach. Tancred handed her down onto the shore without comment and pulled her in lengthy strides along the water's edge.

Arianne was gasping for breath by the time they reached the place where Tancred's ship was anchored. On the beach, a small boat with six men awaited Tancred's arrival.

Tightening his grip on Arianne, Tancred moved

forward. In a flash, Richard stepped out from behind the rocks and with him, over a dozen of his own men.

"Halt there!" he called to Tancred. "Release my wife and take to your ship."

Tancred took two more steps then stopped, pulling Arianne to his side. "I'm taking her with me. She will be my guarantee of safety from Henry and from your wrath."

"Try to take her and you will know more of my wrath than you had ever thought possible." Richard's words held a deadly tone.

Arianne's heart pounded at the scene unfolding before her. If she could not do something to assuage the tempers of these men, she could well be a widow by nightfall.

"I beg of you, Tancred," she whispered then turned to her husband. "Please, Richard, let this thing be at peace between you. Your brother knows naught of God and His mercy. You are God's witness to that mercy and love. If you do not show forth the light of God's truth, how will Tancred come to know it?"

"I am not his salvation," Richard replied, his eyes never leaving Tancred's stony face.

"'Tis true you are not his salvation, but you have knowledge of the way to that salvation that has been forsaken or forgotten by your brother."

Richard's face was etched in pain. The truth of Arianne's words affected him in a way he couldn't explain. For so many years he had carried blind hatred for the man before him, certain that Tancred had been responsible for the deaths of their parents. But maybe Arianne was right. Perhaps Tancred had no responsibility in the murders. Maybe it was time to let go of his hatred.

"King Henry has etched in the walls of his palaces words

that are most eloquent and true," Richard murmured. Tancred and Arianne waited in silence for him to continue. "It reads, 'He who does not give what he has will not get what he wants.' I must give up my hatred in order to find the peace that I desire."

"Will you let me pass?" Tancred asked. His grip tightened on Arianne, causing her to wince painfully.

"Not with my wife. You may leave and I freely give you your men and ship, but you will never leave English soil with Arianne. She is my wife and will remain here with me," Richard stated firmly.

Arianne held her breath, wondering what Tancred's reply would be. Without a word, Tancred pulled Arianne with him as he began to edge around Richard.

"I am no fool, dear brother. You could easily send your men to cut me down. With Arianne, I will have my assurance that you will behave in a gentlemanly manner and honor your word."

"You will not take her," Richard restated and the sound of his sword being freed from the scabbard rang clear for all ears.

Tancred stopped as Richard raised his sword, but it was Arianne who stunned them both into silence. With a strength she'd not known she possessed, Arianne wrenched herself free from Tancred's grip and threw herself between Tancred and Richard.

"You will be no better than him," Arianne whispered desperately to her husband. "You cannot murder him, for his soul will haunt you for all eternity. You will always know that he died without God's forgiveness and that had you been merciful, Tancred might have lived to accept God."

The tip of Richard's sword pointed to Arianne's breast. Dumfounded at her words, he didn't know how to respond.

Tancred, too, stood frozen in place. He was mesmerized by the young woman who so gallantly defended his right to live. He was troubled by her words of God's forgiveness, but he couldn't bring himself to betray the longing they stirred within.

"Please," Arianne begged, as the wind tore at her copper hair. Several strands fell across the raised blade, bringing Richard back to his senses.

"Go," Richard told his brother, lowering the sword slowly.

Tancred reached out for Arianne, but before Richard could move, Arianne turned to face her brother-in-law.

"Nay, Tancred," she whispered. "I will not go with you freely, and you will not force me. There is something of value within you; something yet redeemable and good. You are harsh and troubled, and there is much that you must confess before God, but you have my forgiveness for the evil you have done me. Let that be your starting place. Remember Henry's words with respect for their value, even if you cannot respect the man."

Tancred stared at Arianne and saw compassion in her eyes. It was the first time in many years that he had experienced such sincerity and generosity of spirit. He quickly stepped back as though being too near her caused him greater pain. Lifting his face to meet Richard's, he saw that Arianne's words had also humbled his brother.

Arianne moved into Richard's waiting arms. She relished the warmth and safety found there and sighed with relief as he pulled her close.

"And what of you, brother?" Tancred suddenly found

his tongue. "Have I your forgiveness as well?"

"Do you seek it?" Richard questioned without sarcasm.

Tancred was taken aback only for a moment. Richard's forgiveness was something he desired almost more than the reinstatement of his land and title. How could he have been so blinded by fury and hatred to have expected his brother to lie, even give his life up, in order to free him from exile?

"I came here to seek my freedom," Tancred answered and the sadness in his voice was not lost on the young couple before him. "I know naught of the peace you know in God. Mayhap in time, it will be shown to me in the same manner it has been revealed to you. Mayhap I will lay to rest the demons from the past." He paused and shook his head. "I know naught what manner of woman you have married, brother, but she is like none I have ever known. Do not consider her lightly, for there are few like her."

Richard smiled down at the woman in his arms. "Aye," he whispered, "I know it well."

Tancred turned to leave and then, remembering his brother's question, paused. "I did not slay our parents. Perhaps my negligence of them somehow aided in the deed, but not because I chose it to be so. I did not kill them."

Richard sobered and nodded. "I believe you." Deep peace filled his heart as Richard realized he meant the words in full.

"Then will you give me your forgiveness?" Tancred questioned.

"Aye," Richard replied. "You are free from my hatred. I desire nothing more than you live out your days in peace and in the true understanding of God's love." Then Richard added, "Will you forgive me?"

Tancred said nothing for several moments. He saw a truly great man in his brother, and it was difficult for him to realize that had things been different, they might have stood side by side.

"Aye," Tancred said. "You have my forgiveness." Without another word, he turned and waded into the water. There was no fear that Richard would have him murdered or waylaid en route to his exile. After a brief salute, Tancred climbed into the boat and never looked back.

eighteen

That night, Arianne sat deep in thought beside the hearth in their bed chamber. Staring into the fire, she wondered at the differences between Richard and his brother. What drove men to such contrasts? A noise behind her caused Arianne to look up only to find Richard's intense green eyes watching her.

"You creep more silently than the night itself," Arianne mused, then felt a warm blush edge her cheeks. Suddenly she felt very shy. The look on Richard's face stirred her heart and quickened her breath.

Richard crossed the room and pulled his wife against him. "I've missed you more dearly than anything else these walls could offer." He lowered his face to her hair and breathed in the unmistakable scent of Arianne's favorite soap. The long coppery curls wrapped around his fingers as he plunged his hands into the bulk. "You are perfection on earth," he sighed.

Arianne lifted her face from his chest with a mischievous grin. "I was thinking much the same of you," she admitted, causing Richard to chuckle.

"'Tis most grateful I am to have married a cunning, intelligent woman. Milady, you are a most precious jewel to me, and as long as I live, I will love no other."

Arianne reached up her hand to touch the neatly trimmed beard. "My heart's true love," she whispered.

Her brown eyes held the promise of a life of love, and

in their reflection Richard found all that he had ever longed for. Gently, as though afraid the spell would be broken, Richard lowered his lips to Arianne's and kissed her with all the longing that had been denied them both. With his world once again at peace, Richard intended to concentrate on the fact that he and Arianne were yet newly wed.

Weeks blended into months and Arianne knew a peace and contentment that was like nothing she'd ever imagined possible. Life with Richard was so much more than the routine tasks of the day. She never failed to be warmed by the glint in his eyes when he lifted his gaze from the company of his men to take note of her when she entered a room. Nor could she begin to understand the wonder of lying in his arms at night, feeling the rhythmic beat of his heart against her hand as it lay in casual possession of Richard's chest.

Forgotten were the days of her father's brutality and rage, for in Richard's care, Arianne knew nothing more than the firm correction in his voice when she erred and the loving approval of his smile when she caused him great pride in something new she'd learned. There were still unanswered questions about his parents' deaths, but Arianne's only unfulfilled desire was to see her brother, Devon.

"Arianne!" Richard called from the great hall. "Arianne!"

Arianne rose from her work in the solarium and went in search of her husband. Matilda met her in the hall with a smile broader than the river that flowed nearby.

"Your Grace," she said with a light curtsey. "The duke will be most pleased to see you."

"And what has he to show me this time?" Arianne questioned with teasing in her voice. "The last time he arrived home with this much excitement, he brought me news that the King intended to receive us as guests. Pray tell, what could top that?"

Matilda smiled knowingly but said nothing as she hurried Arianne to the stone stairway. Arianne knew better than to question her maid, for when Matilda wanted to keep something to herself, she did so quite well.

Arianne lifted her skirts ever so slightly and in a most unladylike fashion hurried her descent. She hadn't reached the final step, however, before Richard reached out and lifted her into the air. Swinging her round and round until Arianne begged him to put her down, Richard couldn't contain his joy.

"What have you done this time?" Arianne asked with a grin.

"I have brought you a gift, milady," he replied, taking her hand in his own. "And I believe it will meet wholeheartedly with your approval."

"'Most everything you do meets with my approval," replied Arianne.

Richard raised an eyebrow and stopped in mid-step. "Only 'most everything?"

"Well, there was that problem with the puppies you brought into our bed chamber," Arianne laughed, remembering an incident several days past.

"Who knew they could move so fast!" Richard said in his defense. "Besides, I caught them all again, didn't I?"

"True," Arianne nodded, trying to be serious, "but not before they'd tracked mud all over the room and threatened to raise the roof with their yipping and howls."

"Well, this time there will be no tracking of mud and no yipping or howling," Richard promised, pulling Arianne along with him once again.

"We shall see," she mused with a wifely air.

Entering the great hall, Arianne could see that nothing looked amiss. She glanced up curiously to catch her husband's eye, but Richard refused to give away his secret.

"Sit here," he commanded lovingly and assisted Arianne into a chair. "Now close your eyes."

Arianne's brow wrinkled ever so slightly and a smile played at the edge of her lips. "The last time you told me to do that—" Her words were cut off, however, when Richard insisted she be obedient.

"Hurry, now, or you'll spoil everything."

Arianne shook her head in mock exasperation, but nevertheless closed her eyes.

"Are they closed tight?" Richard asked her.

"Yes," she replied. "They are closed as tight as I can close them. Now will you please tell me what's going on."

"In a minute. I've almost got it ready," Richard answered.

"Remember your promise," teased Arianne while she waited in her self-imposed darkness.

"What promise was that my dear?"

"No mud, no yipping, no howls," she said, laughing in spite of her struggle to remain serious.

"I promise," came a voice that did not belong to her husband. "You will get no such scene from me."

Arianne's heart skipped a beat. Her eyes flashed open wide to greet the vaguely familiar face of her brother. "Devon!" she cried and threw herself into his waiting arms.

"You are an enchanting sight for such weary eyes," Devon said, squeezing Arianne tightly. "We've been separated far too long."

"I can't believe you are truly here," Arianne replied and stepped back to search the room for Richard. He was leaning against the table with his arms folded against his chest and a broad grin on his face.

"I told you it would meet with your approval."

"Richard, you are indeed a wonder. However did you find him, and whatever possessed you to bring him here?" Arianne asked, returning her gaze to Devon.

"You spoke of him so often, I thought he might as well be here in body, as well as spirit. Henry had him in service elsewhere, but then Henry has always had a soft spot in his heart for me." Richard seemed quite pleased with himself, and Arianne broke away from Devon's side to embrace her husband.

"You are a man of many talents, Duke DuBonnet," she murmured against his ear before placing a light kiss upon his cheek.

Richard pulled her close, winking at Devon over her shoulder. "I knew this would make up for the puppies," he grinned.

Devon and Arianne both laughed at this. "I will never bring up the subject of the puppies again," Arianne promised. Her heart was overflowing with the love and happiness she felt at that moment. "How long can you stay, Devon?" she questioned, knowing that she might not like the answer.

"That depends on you," Devon replied with a knowing glance at Richard.

"On me?" Arianne's confusion was clear.

"Aye," Devon said with a nod. "How long will you have me?"

Arianne moved to her brother, pulling Richard along with her. "I'd have you here forever," she answered and looped her free arm through Devon's.

"That might be pressing it, my love." Richard's voice held a tone of teasing. "Why not just until King Henry rewards him with lands of his own for the service he's so faithfully given."

Arianne could not have looked more pleased. "Truly?" she asked. "Truly, Henry is going to bestow a title upon him?"

"'Tis true enough," Richard replied. "But, until then, Devon is our guest and—"

Devon interrupted, "And your most humble servant, milady."

"Nay," Arianne said, shaking her head. "Never that. Just a long lost soul who has finally come home to those who love him." The pleasure on her face was clear. "And, for that I truly thank God, King Henry, and my most tender-hearted husband."

Later that evening, Arianne sought out Richard in their bed chamber. He had just finished with his bath and was donning one of the lined tunics she'd made for him.

"These have worked like a wonder," he commented. "I don't think I've ever had a chance to thank you properly for the thoughtfulness of your work."

Arianne smiled. "It was a task I took to with a glad heart, for I knew it would be well received."

"Aye, that it has. I see that Devon, too, has been well received."

"Oh, most assuredly. Richard, I cannot tell you what it means to me to have him here. I have missed him sorely and look forward to rekindling ou friendship. Already he has shared many great stories ɔí his adventures."

"What of your father?" Richard asked softly. "Has he given you word of him?"

"Nay," Arianne replied and walked away to the window. "But, neither have I asked. 'Tis a difficult matter. I am glad my father is not alone and I pray his new wife makes him happy. I hold him no malice. I simply wish to forget the sorrow."

"No doubt your mother's passing grieved him in a way that left him unable to deal with his children properly," Richard said from behind her.

"Mayhap he grieved that she never loved him," Arianne replied without turning. "He always knew, and in spite of the fact that he never told her, I believe my father loved my mother."

"Hopefully things will be different this time. Devon tells me your step-mother will bear him a child."

Arianne turned and stared at her husband in surprise. "Is this true?"

"Aye," Richard said. He sat down on the edge of the bed and awaited Arianne's response to the news.

"When?" she questioned so softly that Richard nearly missed the word.

"Devon tells me the babe should be born after Hocktide at the end of Easter."

Arianne completely surprised Richard as a mischievous grin spread across her face. "Good," she said, folding her arms against her body. "I shall beat her by a fortnight, at least."

Richard stared dumbly for a moment, not fully understanding the news his wife had just shared.

Arianne continued before he could question her. "Matilda tells me we should expect to become parents in the spring." Anticipation and joy radiated from Arianne's countenance.

Richard shook his head as if trying to awaken from a

dream. "Parents?" he questioned, coming to his feet. "You're going to give me a child? How long have you known?"

Arianne giggled like a little girl with a secret. "I've only just learned this myself, Your Grace. But you will admit, 'tis a surprise that ranks at least as high as puppies."

At this Richard's laughter filled the chamber. He lifted Arianne in his arms and hugged her tightly. "Madam, it most assuredly surpasses all my other surprises. I am most pleased at this news. God has given me all that a man could want and then doubled it. My joy truly knows no bounds."

Arianne sighed against the warmth of her husband. "I feel the same, and had I not been forced by the king into marriage with you, I would never have known what a truly remarkable man you are. And had you been any less remarkable, I would never have known what true love was about. You have given me much, Richard. A child, a home, a loving companion for life, but even more: you opened my eyes to the love of God. A love that reigns here," she whispered and placed his hand over her heart, "because one man heard the soft call of His master's voice above the roar of men's."

"Sweet Arianne," Richard murmured, lifting his hand to cup her chin. "In the stillness of His love, we will heed His call together. All of our lives we will face the future knowing that He has seen what is to come and walks the path beside us. There will be no kingdom divided or heart destroyed, so long as we keep our steps with Him."

A Letter To Our Readers

Dear Reader:

In order that we might better contribute to your reading enjoyment, we would appreciate your taking a few minutes to respond to the following questions. When completed, please return to the following:

Rebecca Germany, Editor
Heartsong Presents
P.O. Box 719
Uhrichsville, Ohio 44683

1. Did you enjoy reading *A Kingdom Divided*?
   ❏ Very much. I would like to see more books
     by this author!
   ❏ Moderately
     I would have enjoyed it more if _____

   _____

2. Are you a member of *Heartsong Presents*? Yes No
   If no, where did you purchase this book? _____

   _____

3. What influenced your decision to purchase this
   book? (Check those that apply.)

   ❏ Cover   ❏ Back cover copy

   ❏ Title   ❏ Friends

   ❏ Publicity   ❏ Other _____

4. On a scale from 1 (poor) to 10 (superior), please rate the following elements.

___Heroine ___Plot

___Hero ___Inspirational theme

___Setting ___Secondary characters

5. What settings would you like to see covered in *Heartsong Presents* books?

_____

_____

6. What are some inspirational themes you would like to see treated in future books?_____

_____

_____

7. Would you be interested in reading other *Heartsong Presents* titles? ❏ Yes ❏ No

8. Please check your age range:
❏ Under 18 ❏ 18-24 ❏ 25-34
❏ 35-45 ❏ 46-55 ❏ Over 55

9. How many hours per week do you read? ————

Name _____

Occupation _____

Address _____

City _____ State _____ Zip _____

WESTERN ROMANCE FROM

Janelle Jamison

___*A Place to Belong*—Magdelena Intissar is not about to let Garrett
Lucas drag her from her childhood home to rejoin the father who had
deserted her when she was eight years old. But Garrett—and God—
have other plans. HP19 $2.95

___*Perfect Love*—Beautiful, petite Lillie Philips has always had her
own way. Then tragedy struck and she slipped into an increasing
depression. Can she risk loving and trusting a man like Dr. Daniel
Monroe? HP40 $2.95

___*Tender Journeys*—Not since her parents died has Jenny Oberling
known love. David Monroe determines to marry Jenny, but Jenny's
guardian has other plans. As David frantically works against time, he
fears the worst: He may be too late to free Jenny. HP47 $2.95

___*The Willing Heart*—Alexandra Stewart must choose between
starvation and salvation. Faced with an impossible ultimatum, Zandy
comes to discover the true reason why Riley Dawson was sent into her
world. . .and the hidden treasure of a willing heart. HP63 $2.95

___*Beyond Today*—Amidst the hard and unpredictable life on the
Kansas prairie, Amy Carmichael has learned to never live beyond
today. That changes, though, when she meets Tyler Andrews, the new
circuit rider. But will Tyler return Amy's love, or is he more attracted
to Amy's twin sister Angie? HP88 $2.95

Send to: Heartsong Presents Reader's Service
P.O. Box 719
Uhrichsville, Ohio 44683

Please send me the items checked above. I am enclosing
$_____(please add $1.00 to cover postage and handling
per order. OH add 6.25% tax. NJ add 6% tax.).
Send check or money order, no cash or C.O.D.s, please.
To place a credit card order, call 1-800-847-8270.

NAME _____

ADDRESS _____

CITY/STATE _____ ZIP_____
JAMISON

···· Hearts ♥ng ····

Any 12 *Heartsong Presents* titles for only $26.95 *

HISTORICAL ROMANCE IS CHEAPER BY THE DOZEN!

Buy any assortment of twelve *Heartsong Presents* titles and save 25% off of the already discounted price of $2.95 each!

*plus $1.00 shipping and handling per order and sales tax where applicable.

HEARTSONG PRESENTS TITLES AVAILABLE NOW:

__HP 1 A TORCH FOR TRINITY, *Colleen L. Reece*
__HP 2 WILDFLOWER HARVEST, *Colleen L. Reece*
__HP 7 CANDLESHINE, *Colleen L. Reece*
__HP 8 DESERT ROSE, *Colleen L. Reece*
__HP 11 RIVER OF FIRE, *Jacquelyn Cook*
__HP 12 COTTONWOOD DREAMS, *Norene Morris*
__HP 15 WHISPERS ON THE WIND, *Maryn Langer*
__HP 16 SILENCE IN THE SAGE, *Colleen L. Reece*
__HP 19 A PLACE TO BELONG, *Janelle Jamison*
__HP 20 SHORES OF PROMISE, *Kate Blackwell*
__HP 23 GONE WEST, *Kathleen Karr*
__HP 24 WHISPERS IN THE WILDERNESS, *Colleen L. Reece*
__HP 27 BEYOND THE SEARCHING RIVER, *Jacquelyn Cook*
__HP 28 DAKOTA DAWN, *Lauraine Snelling*
__HP 31 DREAM SPINNER, *Sally Laity*
__HP 32 THE PROMISED LAND, *Kathleen Karr*
__HP 35 WHEN COMES THE DAWN, *Brenda Bancroft*
__HP 36 THE SURE PROMISE, *JoAnn A. Grote*
__HP 39 RAINBOW HARVEST, *Norene Morris*
__HP 40 PERFECT LOVE, *Janelle Jamison*
__HP 43 VEILED JOY, *Colleen L. Reece*
__HP 44 DAKOTA DREAM, *Lauraine Snelling*
__HP 47 TENDER JOURNEYS, *Janelle Jamison*
__HP 48 SHORES OF DELIVERANCE, *Kate Blackwell*
__HP 51 THE UNFOLDING HEART, *JoAnn A. Grote*
__HP 52 TAPESTRY OF TAMAR, *Colleen L. Reece*
__HP 55 TREASURE OF THE HEART, *JoAnn A. Grote*
__HP 56 A LIGHT IN THE WINDOW, *Janelle Jamison*
__HP 59 EYES OF THE HEART, *Maryn Langer*
__HP 60 MORE THAN CONQUERORS, *Kay Cornelius*
__HP 63 THE WILLING HEART, *Janelle Jamison*

(If ordering from this page, please remember to include it with the order form.)

·······• Presents ·······

__HP 64 CROWS'-NESTS AND MIRRORS, *Colleen L. Reece*
__HP 67 DAKOTA DUSK, *Lauraine Snelling*
__HP 68 RIVERS RUSHING TO THE SEA, *Jacquelyn Cook*
__HP 71 DESTINY'S ROAD, *Janelle Jamison*
__HP 72 SONG OF CAPTIVITY, *Linda Herring*
__HP 75 MUSIC IN THE MOUNTAINS, *Colleen L. Reece*
__HP 76 HEARTBREAK TRAIL, *VeraLee Wiggins*
__HP 79 AN UNWILLING WARRIOR, *Andrea Shaar*
__HP 80 PROPER INTENTIONS, *Dianne L. Christner*
__HP 83 MARTHA MY OWN, *VeraLee Wiggins*
__HP 84 HEART'S DESIRE, *Paige Winship Dooly*
__HP 87 SIGN OF THE BOW, *Kay Cornelius*
__HP 88 BEYOND TODAY, *Janelle Jamison*
__HP 91 SIGN OF THE EAGLE, *Kay Cornelius*
__HP 92 ABRAM MY LOVE, *VeraLee Wiggins*
__HP 95 SIGN OF THE DOVE, *Kay Cornelius*
__HP 96 FLOWER OF SEATTLE, *Colleen L. Reece*
__HP 99 ANOTHER TIME...ANOTHER PLACE, *Bonnie L. Crank*
__HP100 RIVER OF PEACE, *Janelle Burnham*
__HP103 LOVE'S SHINING HOPE, *JoAnn A. Grote*
__HP104 HAVEN OF PEACE, *Carol Mason Parker*
__HP107 PIONEER LEGACY, *Norene Morris*
__HP108 LOFTY AMBITIONS, *Diane L. Christner*
__HP111 A KINGDOM DIVIDED, *Tracie J. Peterson*
__HP112 CAPTIVES OF THE CANYON, *Colleen L. Reece*

Great Inspirational Romance at a Great Price!

Heartsong Presents books are inspirational romances in contemporary and historical settings, designed to give you an enjoyable, spirit-lifting reading experience. You can choose from 112 wonderfully written titles from some of today's best authors like Colleen L. Reece, Brenda Bancroft, Janelle Jamison, and many others.

When ordering quantities less than twelve, above titles are $2.95 each.

| SEND TO: Heartsong Presents Reader's Service |
| P.O. Box 719, Uhrichsville, Ohio 44683 |

Please send me the items checked above. I am enclosing $_____.
(please add $1.00 to cover postage per order. OH add 6.25% tax. NJ add 6%.). Send check or money order, no cash or C.O.D.s, please.
To place a credit card order, call 1-800-847-8270.

NAME _____

ADDRESS _____

CITY/STATE_____ ZIP _____

HPS FEBRUARY

Hearts♥ng Presents
Love Stories Are Rated G!

That's for godly, gratifying, and of course, great! If you love a thrilling love story, but don't appreciate the sordidness of popular paperback romances, **Heartsong Presents** is for you. In fact, **Heartsong Presents** is the *only inspirational romance book club*, the only one featuring love stories where Christian faith is the primary ingredient in a marriage relationship.

Sign up today to receive your first set of four, never before published Christian romances. Send no money now; you will receive a bill with the first shipment. You may cancel at any time without obligation, and if you aren't completely satisfied with any selection, you may return the books for an immediate refund!

Imagine. . .four new romances every month—two historical, two contemporary—with men and women like you who long to meet the one God has chosen as the love of their lives. . .all for the low price of $9.97 postpaid.

To join, simply complete the coupon below and mail to the address provided. **Heartsong Presents** romances are rated G for another reason: They'll arrive *Godspeed!*

YES! Sign me up for Hearts♥ng!

NEW MEMBERSHIPS WILL BE SHIPPED IMMEDIATELY!
Send no money now. We'll bill you only $9.97 post-paid with your first shipment of four books. Or for faster action, call toll free !-800-847-8270.

NAME _____

ADDRESS _____

CITY _____ STATE _____ ZIP _____

MAIL TO: HEARTSONG PRESENTS, P.O. Box 791, Uhrichsville, Ohio 44683

YES 8-94